Fatal Lady

Also by Rae Foley
in Thorndike Large Print ®

The Shelton Conspiracy
Back Door to Death
Call It Accident
It's Murder, Mr. Potter
Death and Mr. Potter
The Last Gamble

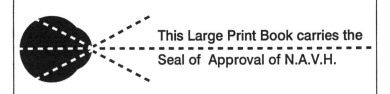

Fatal Lady

A Mr. Potter Mystery

Rae Foley

Thorndike Press • Thorndike, Maine

Published in 1994 by arrangement with Golden West Literary Agency.

The characters, places, incidents, and situations in this book are imaginary and have no relation to any person, place, or actual happening.

Thorndike Large Print ® General Series.

The tree indicium is a trademark of Thorndike Press.

The text of this Large Print edition is unabridged. Other aspects of the book may vary from the original edition.

Set in 16 pt. News Plantin by Minnie B. Raven.

Printed in the United States on acid-free, high opacity paper. ∞

Library of Congress Cataloging in Publication Data

Foley, Rae, 1900–
    Fatal lady : a Mr. Potter mystery / by Rae Foley.
      p.   cm.
    ISBN 0-7862-0027-8 (alk. paper: lg. print)
    1. Large type books. I. Title.
    [PS3507.E5725F3   1994]
    813'.54—dc20   93-26722

For Lois — *again*
With a bow to Norma

ONE

In response to the light tap on her horn a man peered out, gave her a quick look and opened the gates. In the parking area she locked her car — "Always leave your car locked," they had warned her on that first day, three years ago — and took a long breath before turning to the main building.

"What a beautiful place!" people exclaimed the first time they saw Wentworth. The buildings of gray limestone were gracious in design, with ivy climbing up the walls. The scarlet leaves of October crept almost over the windows, almost concealed the bars that shone brightly in the sparkling autumn air. The gardens, brilliant now with asters and chrysanthemums, were famous.

Here and there, people strolled along the paths, leisurely people, fortunate people to have this loveliness to enjoy. But no one walked alone. For each stroller there was a watchful attendant.

She scanned the passing faces, but Cass wasn't there and she went swiftly up the three shallow steps of the main building, out of the sun, into the clear shadowless light of the reception room. Even here there was

7

no trace of the real nature of the place. Dr. Halstead had strong convictions about the importance of surroundings, and he had the money to carry them out. There were deep rugs on the floor, bright chintz at the windows and on chairs and couches. There were flowers in vases and in bowls on the tables. Cass wasn't here, either.

A girl in a blue wool dress — Dr. Halstead dispensed with uniforms whenever possible — looked up from the chart she was working on and smiled a greeting.

"Wonderful day, isn't it? Do you want to consult Dr. Halstead this morning?"

"Why?" asked the bleak voice. "He always says 'no change.' "

The receptionist's smile deepened with professional brightness. "Well, I always say no news is good news."

"Why?" Janet asked again.

The smile faded out uncertainly. "I think you'll find your brother in the game room."

The big sunlit game room, through the archway in the south wall, was one of Dr. Halstead's show pieces. Next to the superb food and the gardens, the game room at Wentworth was the reason for such fantastic prices being paid without serious complaint. There were four people playing bridge at one table, someone desultorily working a jigsaw puzzle, two young men playing Ping-pong. Cass wasn't there, either.

She was about to go into the library when there was a cry of anger. One of the Ping-pong players had lunged at the other. A white-coated attendant, who had been reading a newspaper, moved quickly, separated the two struggling young men, and led one of them away, talking in a soothing voice but holding him firmly by the arm. No one else paid any attention.

Janet shivered and went into the library. Cass was sunk in a deep chair, reading, so absorbed that he was unaware of her presence. Her throat tightened as she looked at him. His hair was almost white. There were deep lines from the corners of his mouth to his chin. His round face had thinned out, had grown gaunt and stern. For the first time she saw his strong family resemblance to Thornton. It would be hard now for anyone to find a trace of Cass the playboy.

He looked up and saw her, closed his book and got to his feet.

"Hi, there! Is that a new Katherine Lord creation? You look terrific." He hugged her and kissed her cheek lightly.

"What have you been doing?" she asked and tried too late to stop the words. But what could she say to him? What could she talk about that was safe, that wouldn't hurt? That was why the gulf between them widened steadily. She did not know how to talk to him anymore, how to reach him.

And Cass didn't help. He made no attempt to bridge the gulf. He withdrew, slowly but inexorably, into his own private world, into the thoughts that had whitened his hair — at thirty-three! — and dug bitter lines in his face. And he would not share them with her.

The one time she had made a desperate effort to reach him, to break through his shield of loneliness, he had lashed at her, the Grant temper that had become so notorious flaring in his eyes.

"For God's sake, let me alone! That's all I ask of you. Let me alone. Stop coming here. It's hell for both of us."

She hadn't tried to invade his solitude again, but she hadn't stopped coming to Wentworth. Little by little, they had erected the fragile pretense that the gulf wasn't there, that nothing had changed between them.

Now Cass summoned up the smile that she hated, a smile of self-mockery. "Nice timing," he told her. "I couldn't have staged it better if I had planned it. You caught me improving my mind." He held out the book he had been reading, *The Metamorphoses* of Ovid. "And if

10

that doesn't impress you in a guy who never read beyond the headlines, I don't know what would."

"Good heavens, do I have to contend with two classical scholars in the same family?" Her tone had the proper lightness but the smile touched only her lips, it did not reach her eyes.

"Let's get out of here," he said abruptly, and then carefully rephrased the words. "It's too nice a day to stay indoors."

Why don't you say you hate it? she asked him in her mind. Why don't you tell me what you are really thinking?

They strolled up and down the paths, the sunlight on his white hair that had been so blond four years ago, and talked emptily with sporadic attempts at gaiety that fell of their own weight. They pretended this was only a pleasant garden. They pretended not to notice the people who passed, their eyes too dull, their gestures too feverish, mentally alone but never physically alone. They pretended not to see the white-coated attendant who strolled behind them, never so close as to overhear their conversation, never so far away as to be unable to reach them in an emergency.

Cass walked with her to the parking area and stood watching while she unlocked the car. She looked up unexpectedly and saw his expression, the fierce longing in his eyes. Then his guard was up again. He put his hand on the door after she was at the wheel. Instantly the attendant was on the alert, closing the gap, watchful to see that he did not attempt to escape.

Seeing him, Cass laughed for the first time. His hand tightened. "You can't keep this up, Jan. Don't come back. You only hurt yourself and you can't help me. Why don't you go away and forget all this? Why don't you get married?"

"No takers," she said lightly.

"With your looks? What did the papers call you — the most beautiful debutante of a generation?" The ugly expression returned to his face. "Is it because of me — being here, I mean?"

"Don't be a fool! I just — there's no one —"

"What about Pete? Don't tell me that faithful hound isn't still on your traces."

"Oh, Pete's still around."

"What a doormat! He'd get farther with you if he choked you now and then." He snatched at the words and appeared not to see how the color drained out of her face. "Poor faithful Pete! You lead him a dog's life. But I suppose he likes it or he wouldn't keep on. He was

12

up here yesterday. Once a month like clock-work."

"He's a good and loyal friend," she said, stung into answering his tone rather than his words. "If it weren't for Pete you wouldn't be here now."

"Don't you think," he told her, all pretense stripped away, "I'd rather have had the electric chair?" His voice had risen and the attendant was somehow beside him, smiling but gesturing for her to go on.

She started the car, backed out of the parking area, turned toward the closed gates. As the watchman opened them for her she looked over her shoulder. Cass was walking slowly toward one of the dormitories, as Dr. Halstead liked to call them, and the attendant walked beside him, their arms closely linked.

When she had garaged her car on Second Avenue, she walked the four blocks to Madison and the small shop on 54th Street with its unobtrusive plaque: KATHERINE LORD. On the fifty-minute drive down from Wentworth to New York City she had tried to stem the sick despair she always felt after her visits to Cass, to make herself grapple with the problems of the present, with the life she had carved out for herself after — since Cass had been sent to Wentworth.

13

Automatically she inspected the shop windows, comparing the dresses with those she designed. She paused abruptly and turned back to study an odd color combination, undecided as to whether she liked it or not. Difficult, of course, but for a real brunette it would be dramatic.

That was when she heard the halting step. She whirled around, looking at the people behind her. Then she made herself go on, listening, all her attention bent on catching that sound, the footsteps of a limping man. Again she turned quickly, as though hoping to catch someone off-guard. She must be acting queerly because people noticed her, looked at her face. Someone recognized her and there was a startled comment.

She jerked on dark glasses, too late as usual. They bothered her and she often forgot to wear them, though they gave her a comforting illusion of being completely disguised. After all, it was that unusual combination of pale hair with eyes that were almost black that people were likely to remember.

She found herself hurrying, trying to escape the attention of the curious, and forced herself to slow down. She couldn't run away. As she changed her pace she heard it again, the halting footstep behind her. It was a long time since she had heard it, since she had been

14

aware that she was being followed. But why now?

It was refuge to reach her shop. The door opened onto a long narrow room deeply carpeted in dark gray with walls of a paler gray brocade. At the far end a short staircase led on either side to a shallow balcony, designed for the models who displayed the Katherine Lord dresses. There were several small sofas upholstered in cherry satin, with low tables that held cigarettes, ashtrays and, when the customers were really buying, highballs.

Her eyes made a quick survey of the room. Very effective, she thought in approval. There was no one in the shop. Except for fittings, few of her regular customers appeared in the mornings, though there were always strangers who dropped in and who were usually appalled by the prices.

"For that simple little dress?" they would exclaim.

Katherine Lord's tilted brows would rise and she would move slowly across the room. The customer's eyes would follow her, the beautiful carriage, the subtle line of the dress, the indefinable air of distinction. If she had the money, she usually bought the dress.

At the end of the long room a door concealed in brocaded panels led to the private office. The only sounds came from the ventilator in

15

the wall that opened on the loft floor above, where the Katherine Lord dresses were created. There was the whir of an electric sewing machine, the faint steamy smell of a pressing iron, two voices that identified themselves as belonging to the head saleswoman and a new model.

". . . and don't," the saleswoman was saying, "let Miss Lord catch you coming in here in slacks. The point of the Katherine Lord dresses is to make girls look like girls again and not like beatniks or gunmen's molls. She is bringing glamour back to women, and high time, too. Give men a break. Any man I've ever known prefers making love to a pretty girl rather than comforting himself that in the dark all cats are gray."

The model giggled. "You're awful! Anyhow, I only wore these because —"

"Just don't let it happen again. That's all."

"Okay," the model agreed amiably. "I guess she's pretty hard to please."

"No, she's swell to work for. Too soft, in my opinion. She's a pushover for hard-luck stories. But don't try to put anything over on her. She's got the Grant temper and never forget it."

"Grant?" the model repeated blankly.

"Good lord! Didn't you know? She's really Janet Grant. Katherine Lord is just a sort of trade-mark. Personally, I always thought the prosecution made too much of the Grant temper at the trial. It's like a line of powder, a blinding flash, a roar, and it's all over."

"What trial?"

"Where have you been keeping yourself? Her brother, Cass Grant. The Frederick murder case."

"Jeez! The murderer — well, whadda ya know? Married to that gorgeous girl, Eve Grant. My brother's got all the newspaper pitchers of her in his room. She's his favorite pin-up. Cass Grant. He got off, ditta he? I remember people were sore about it. Playboy Grant, idle young society man, pampered rich, they called him. Guess with all that money he could buy his way out."

"He's in Wentworth for life as a psycho, if you call that getting off. Now try that Gray Dawn, will you? Miss Lord isn't satisfied with the shoulder line."

Janet dropped her head on her hands. Wouldn't it ever stop? The ugliness. The gloating. The gossip. The pain.

She heard the outer door open and the saleswoman said on a long breath, "Oh-oh. Don't bother with the Gray Dawn now. You'll be doing some modeling."

The model apparently peered out of the door on the balcony, a thing they were strictly forbidden to do. "Who's the customer? She's real good-looking for her age, isn't she?"

"She ought to be. Twenty years ago, she was a famous beauty, one of the Lorton sisters. That is Mrs. Maitland Frederick."

"The widow of the man Cass Grant murdered? Well, whadda ya know?"

Janet discovered that she was shaking. She pushed back her chair and went out of the office, head high, shoulders squared. The woman who turned to her was in her late forties, rather heavy but with traces of great beauty. Automatically, Janet noticed with approval the subtle lines of the black suit, the chic hat, the small fur scarf and wondered who dressed Mrs. Frederick. Someone, obviously, who knew her job.

For an endless moment they stood looking at each other, the older woman with searching curiosity, the girl as though braced for a blow. Then Mrs. Frederick held out her hand.

"It has been a long time, Janet."

The girl reluctantly touched the outstretched hand, which tightened on hers and then released it.

"A delightful shop." Mrs. Frederick was a casual acquaintance making polite conversation. "I hear wonderful things about it."

The lighting in the Katherine Lord shop was soft and becoming to women but Janet

18

could see that the firm line of the older woman's jaw had begun to sag, that there were faint crow's-feet at the corners of her eyes, a weary droop to the lips, her hair had turned white. Janet made no effort to sustain the conversation. Mrs. Frederick sank down on one of the satin couches and lighted a cigarette from the box on the table with its initials in silver: K. L.

"I came in because I wanted to speak to you on business. I want to relinquish my lease. There's no sense in having the house stand vacant, but I've never been able to go back there. When I'm not traveling I have some comfortable rooms I keep all the year round at the Plaza. Can you release me?"

"You'll have to consult my cousin, Thornton Grant. My father left him in full charge of our business affairs." Janet could not keep the bitterness out of her voice.

"I always liked your father," Mrs. Frederick said, "but I'm afraid he was a very unforgiving man. Anyhow, I'm sure he wanted to do what he thought was right, what seemed best at the time — for everyone concerned."

She looked at the girl's face. How lovely she was, unforgettable with that smooth fair hair and the enormous dark eyes. The eyes seemed almost too big now in the face that had grown so thin.

"Your poor father," she said gently, "was a victim, of course, a tragic victim of circumstances. As I am. As you are. Even — Cass."

"Even Cass," Janet said, feeling the anger rise in her, lick along her veins. "Even Cass."

"They weren't worth it," Mrs. Frederick said abruptly, startling herself by her own violence. "Maitland and Eve. They weren't worth it! My dear, when I see what it has done to you — oh, you're prettier than ever, I don't mean that — but so barricaded, so untrusting — you've got to learn to put it behind you. Forget it. Build a new life."

"That's what Cass told me this morning."

"It's good advice."

"And what am I to do about Cass? Put him behind me, too? Forget him? Let him stay there forever, rotting slowly away?"

"But, after all, he's better off there than he would be — outside."

"He's as sane as I am," Janet said hotly. "I'll not rest until I've proved that and had him released."

The older woman seized Janet's arm, her hand clenching so tightly that her kid glove split along the seam. "Leave things as they are. Cass escaped the electric chair by a miracle."

"A miracle called Pete Russlin."

"Oh, you mean the young lawyer. Do be

20

grateful for so much."

"Grateful? A mental institution for all his life. I can't bear it. I tell you, I can't bear it. And he can't much longer. How long do you think it will be before he is really mad?"

"Stop it." The words were firm but there was only kindness in Mrs. Frederick's manner. "Believe me, my dear, I understand how you feel. I have no bitterness toward Cass, no feeling of vengeance. But just the same —"

"Well?"

Mrs. Frederick ignored Janet's hostility. "Leave him where he is, my dear. He may be sane, as you believe, but that doesn't alter the fact that he is dangerous."

TWO

Those three things — Cass's white hair, the halting step behind her, and Mrs. Frederick's visit — broke the ice jam that held Janet in a state of suspended animation.

That afternoon she telephoned Thornton Grant and, in spite of his unconcealed reluctance, made an appointment with him for five-thirty. It was typical of Thornton, she thought, that his own cousin had to make an appointment with him. Not that Thornton was ever pressed for time. He spent his days in reading and writing scholarly little essays on Greek and Latin poets, chiefly for his own amusement. Now and then, he brought out, at his own expense, a new translation of some minor Latin poet.

As she arranged for the head saleswoman to show one of her customers the coral chiffon and the black and white dinner dress — "It's all wrong for her but she is bound to want it" — she thought bitterly that Thornton had no need to placate aging women who wanted to look young. The two Grant brothers had inherited their father's railroad fortune and had added to it. Thornton's father had married early in life. He was ten years older than Cass, sixteen years older than Janet.

The cousins had never had a close bond between them, partly because of their age difference, partly because they were wholly unlike. There was no open enmity, just indifference flavored with disapproval. Thornton was the only one of the Grants to escape the notorious Grant temper.

Janet's father had married much later. He had been his mother's darling and she had managed successfully to disrupt her younger son's matrimonial plans for years, until Janet's mother appeared on the scene. Like Janet, she had been tall and slim, with hair that was the palest gold. Like Janet, too, she had had long black eyes, startling against the fairness of her hair. But her gaiety, not subdued even by her possessive mother-in-law, was not like Janet. It was like Cass. A bubbling gaiety that had been snuffed out the day Cass brought Eve home without warning and his mother had toppled over and died of a heart attack.

From the beginning Cass's marriage had been ill-fated, Janet thought. Her father had never forgiven his daughter-in-law for the shock that had killed his wife, though none of them had ever guessed that she had a heart condition.

After the murder of Maitland Frederick, when Cass barely escaped the electric chair

23

and was sent to a state asylum, his father had made a new will. The money belonging to Cass and Janet was to be handled by Thornton, who was given considerable latitude. The amount to be turned over to Janet was left entirely to his discretion. But Cass was to receive only a small monthly income, barely subsistence, unless his name should be cleared.

Having left on record his opinion of his son's guilt, he, too, had died of a heart attack. He had, Janet suspected, welcomed death.

Since the psychiatrist called by Pete Russlin had declared Cass insane, and an all-male jury had, surprisingly, agreed, Janet had found it impossible to live on the meager allowance Thornton gave her and still pay the exorbitant sum required by Wentworth. That transfer to Wentworth from the state asylum was Pete's triumph, though he had suffered for months from the bitter protests of the public. He had been the target for newspaper editorials that dealt with equal justice for all and the inequity of privilege for the rich.

Janet had capitalized on her flair for clothes, had begun to design dresses and had managed to make a success of her enterprise. But the business was too new, the expenses entailed in starting it were too high. She had to have more money.

She prepared carefully for the coming

interview, studied the French knit suit, pulled on the absurd hat that set off her shining smooth hair, and then remembered to put on the dark glasses that concealed her eyes. She must hold on to her temper. Whatever happened, she must not lose her temper.

Thornton occupied two floors of a small house on Murray Hill. A white-coated houseman opened the door and smiled at her.

"Nice to see you again, Miss Janet."

"You're looking well, Jackson."

"Yes'm. Always well. Just the same. Nothing changes much here."

Nothing at all seemed to have changed, Janet thought, as she looked around the familiar drawing room out of which a short flight of stairs led to the second floor, where Thornton had his study and his bedroom. Everything was in good taste, many of the pieces had belonged to his parents, it was all comfortable and pleasant to look at. It just didn't seem lived in. But Thornton's real life, of course, was spent among his books.

In a few minutes he would come down the stairs, walking with his usual deliberation, wearing a maroon velvet jacket, a matching scarf around his throat, his finger in a book as a gentle reminder that she was interrupting him. He would offer her some dry sherry and a biscuit, talk politely and get rid of her as soon as possible. The pattern was familiar. But today, she determined, it would be different. Very different.

There were steps on the stairs and Thornton came down to meet her, walking more briskly than usual, almost running. The quick footsteps of a younger man. The velvet jacket, the scarf, the leather-bound book closed over a finger, were all the same. But Thornton seemed different — younger, more alert. A tall erect man with a fine-boned face like Janet's, a disciplined mouth and the abstracted eyes of a scholar. He looked, Janet thought resentfully, younger than Cass. He was, she reflected in surprise, better-looking. A distinguished man.

He kissed her cheek lightly and smiled approval. "A Katherine Lord creation? It's very becoming."

Janet's brows arched in surprise. Never before had Thornton noticed what she was wearing.

"Scotch? A cocktail? Vodka? Gin? A Manhattan?"

"A martini," Janet said. "Isn't this something new for you, Thornton?"

"A pleasant change." He talked weather until Jackson had brought the cocktails, emptied an ashtray and gone out. He lighted

26

her cigarette. Then he waited. It was up to her now.

"I need some money," she said bluntly.

His face was impassive. "Why?"

"I don't think that really concerns you, Thornton. The money is there. My money."

"My dear girl, you know the terms of the trust. I am helpless."

"You're nothing of the sort. Dad gave you an enormous amount of discretion, at least in regard to my share. You must see that it isn't just. I've had to work like a dog to build the Katherine Lord business. In time, of course, it's going to pay off. But meanwhile — I'm sure Dad never realized —"

Thornton's mouth tightened. "Certainly he didn't realize that you would turn over every penny I gave you — and much more — to keep Cass in that country club. He's living in clover up there, if either of you had the sense to know it."

Janet felt her temper begin to flare and held on to her control. Thornton watched uneasily the face that had grown so rigid. Janet had changed, had become an unknown factor. Before her brother's arrest for murder she had had a springtime quality, a warm eagerness, a wide-eyed trust in the essential goodness of her world. It was all gone now. She was, Thornton reflected, as wary, as untrusting as a caged animal.

"You know your father's reasons as well as I do, Janet. He didn't intend to give you unlimited funds with which to carry on a senseless legal battle to have Cass freed."

Janet drew a long steadying breath. "Thornton, let's get it clear. Cass didn't kill Maitland Frederick. I'll never rest until I get him out of that place. Country club. Dear God! You don't know what it's like. I've simply got to have the money."

Thornton pressed out his cigarette neatly, sipped his cocktail, his eyes intent on her face. "What set you off, Janet, after three years?"

"I've been dazed, I guess. But this morning three things happened. I went up to Wentworth to visit Cass. Do you realize that not a soul ever goes to see him but Pete and me? I found him changed, old. And then I heard the limping man behind me on Fifty-fourth Street."

Thornton gave a small sigh of exasperation. "Your King Charles's head." The lips under the small trim mustache smiled thinly. "The man nobody ever saw."

"And," Janet went on, "I talked to Mrs. Maitland Frederick."

He set down his glass, which struck a thin sweet note. "Mrs. Frederick! Why did you do that?"

28

"I didn't seek her out. She came to the shop."

"What did she want?" he asked sharply. "She should have come to me."

"I told her so. She wants to give up her lease. She's never been back to the house since the — trial. I told her," Janet said dryly, "you handle all my financial affairs."

"She is being very sensible," Thornton said. "Now there will be no further hitch about selling the two houses as a unit."

"I'm not going to sell our house. I'm going to reopen it."

"Good God! That's ridiculous. You don't need that big place. You can't afford to keep it up. Put the past behind you. There's no point in being morbid."

She shook her head. "I'm sick and tired of running away. I'm going back there."

"But, my dear girl —" Thornton began.

He used to call her "My dear child." He didn't like that age difference now. Something was rejuvenating Thornton.

"My dear girl, it's not safe for you. That caretaker of yours — Martin?"

"Marker."

"He has reported half a dozen times that people have broken in."

Janet sat up alertly. "Stolen things, you mean?"

29

"No, nothing appears to be missing. But searching the house, practically ransacking it. I don't like the situation."

Janet's eyes blazed. "Don't you, Thornton? Well, I do. It means there is something in that house to be found. Something hidden. Something, maybe, that would clear Cass. Now nothing would stop me."

Thornton's face seemed as remote as one carved on a mountain. "Don't stir up trouble, Janet. Don't try to — change things. Leave them as they are. Leave Cass where he is. It's better for him. Better — for everyone. Hasn't there been enough suffering?"

"Too much. Much too much. That's why Mrs. Frederick was right. She said they weren't worth it."

"Who weren't?"

"Maitland Frederick and Eve. Their sordid little love affair."

Thornton had never believed in Eve's infidelity. Never for a moment. There was frank hostility in his face now. "We won't discuss it further. No one can dismiss murder simply because the murderer happens to be your spoiled, pampered, self-indulgent brother. As for Eve — what do you suppose would happen to her if you tried to reopen the case, put her back in that unsavory kind of limelight?"

"I couldn't care less. And if anyone can look after herself, it's Eve."

"You're a vindictive little thing, Janet. You look so cool and collected but you are ridden with hatred and you don't seem to realize it. Corroded, poisoned by hatred. Because Eve is such a beautiful girl."

Janet's long eyes opened so wide they seemed to engulf her face. "Jealous of Eve?" she said incredulously.

"I haven't forgotten the trial. I haven't forgotten how you turned on Eve then. Your hysterical attack. That day the Grant temper went off like a time fuse."

He's trying to make me angry, Janet thought in surprise. He wants me to lose my temper. "I didn't attack her because she is beautiful. I attacked her because she lied. She knew who the limping man was and she denied it under oath. And he saw the murder. He could have saved Cass. But Eve cared more about saving her own skin. Her own beautiful skin."

Thornton's beautifully shaped hand rested quietly on the carved arm of his chair. His repose made Janet aware of her own tension, aware that her voice had begun treacherously to climb.

"Janet," he said, his tone quiet and reasonable, infuriatingly reasonable, "by the limping

31

man I assume you mean the window cleaner. The window cleaner whom no one ever hired, whom no one ever saw."

"I saw him. And Eve saw him. I heard him in her room after the murder. And another thing, he's the one who struck her. I don't care what Eve said, it wasn't Cass. He never struck a woman in his life and he worshiped Eve."

"There's no real point in raking up all this, is there?" Thornton said wearily. "Try to look at the situation without prejudice, Janet. Cass always had the Grant temper. He was crazy about Eve. He was also as jealous as hell, pathologically jealous."

"He wasn't jealous of Maitland Frederick. He never knew Eve was having an affair with him. The first he heard of it was when I gave him Mrs. Frederick's message. He didn't believe it."

"Then why did he strangle Frederick?"

"He didn't!"

Thornton began to pace the room with slow, deliberate steps. "I don't understand you. There was no one else. No one with a motive. No one with an opportunity. No one but Cass was in that studio, no one but Cass could even have gotten to the studio, and when he came out Frederick was dead."

"He found him dead."

"That is what he said. But did it take him fifteen minutes to find out? What was he doing in that quarter of an hour?"

"I don't know," Janet said helplessly.

"You know but you won't admit it. Believe me, you would be happier if you would face this thing. I can understand Cass, that jealousy of his, that temper, a sudden impulse — and then it was too late." Thornton reached the end of the room, wheeled, started back. "When he realized how wrong he had been —"

"Wrong?"

"In thinking Eve guilty of misconduct."

"He never thought so, Thornton. That's where he was really wrong. Eve was having an affair. I'd been aware of it for weeks."

"She was loyal, as staunch as steel."

"She lied about the limping man, and she lied about that bruise on her face."

"But look at the way she tried to defend Cass at the trial. Most touching thing I ever witnessed."

"She testified," Janet drawled, "only because she was paid for it. Well paid."

"Janet!"

"Didn't you know that? Didn't you know that Dad gave her a lump sum? Three hundred thousand dollars. You didn't know that, Thornton?"

"No, I didn't know that." He stared at his polished shoe for a moment, looked up, frowning. "My dear, all this is quite pointless, isn't it?"

"You've forgotten the real point. I want some money, my own money, and I want it now. I'm going to get Cass out of Wentworth."

"Not with your father's money. He knew Cass was guilty. Everyone knew. You're the only person who ever believed he could be innocent."

"Pete Russlin believed in him."

"Oh, the young lawyer. I'll grant you he did a brilliant job. But let me remind you, Janet, that Cass never shared Russlin's trust. I'll wager that right now he is still jealous because he met Eve through Russlin in the first place."

"You're evading the issue, Thornton. Are you going to turn over my money?" The "my" was stressed a trifle.

"Be reasonable. Your father left specific instructions —"

"At your discretion," she reminded him.

"You know my opinion. Cass may be sane or he may not, but he's not safe. Let him stay where he is. Forget all this. Give yourself a chance to build a new life. Give Eve a chance to rebuild hers. She has made a fresh start,

34

you know. She has a starring role in Graham Collinge's play, *Fatal Lady*."

At Janet's spontaneous peal of laughter he stopped short. "How you hate her," he said softly.

"No, Mrs. Frederick was right. They weren't worth it. Worth all the trouble they caused, all the heartbreak. But Cass is worth it. Do I get my money?"

"I'm sorry. No."

"Then," Janet said, "I'm going to give the press a good story, one they'll eat up. Frederick murder case reopened. Sister fighting for brother's exoneration and his freedom. And," she added, "I'll tell them it will be difficult because you want to stop me, to prevent my clearing him. I'll tell them that the money is at your disposal and you are hanging onto it, tooth and nail."

"What a particularly filthy thing to do!"

"Isn't it?" she said cheerfully.

"Why can't you believe Cass killed the man? It isn't faith that counts, however touching such faith may be. It's hard fact. You seem to forget that I was there."

"Yes," Janet said thoughtfully, "you were there."

THREE

The telephone was ringing when Janet let herself in at the small apartment on the third floor above her shop on East 54th Street. Pete Russlin, of course. Only a handful of people knew where she lived. Since the trial she had dropped completely out of society and had given no encouragement to the few friends who had remained loyal to her. Of the men who had pursued her so assiduously only Pete remained. The others had dropped away when it became known that she had only a small income at her disposal, that the Grant money was out of her reach.

As she expected, it was Pete's cheerful voice at the end of the wire.

"I've been calling for an hour. I'm thinking of putting you on a leash."

Janet found herself laughing. "You're good for me, Pete."

"What have I been telling you? How about having dinner with me?"

"Not tonight, thanks. I'm so tired."

"A couple of drinks will set you up. Seven-thirty?"

"Well —"

"And wear your best bib and tucker. No

dark glasses. No skulking in dusky corners of obscure restaurants. We're going to see bright lights. We're going to dance."

"Oh, no!"

He heard the panic in her voice. "It's high time," he said firmly. "Seven-thirty." He cut the connection to forestall further objections.

I can't, Janet thought in dismay, go where I'll be stared at, where people will recognize me and whisper. Pete doesn't understand. No, that wasn't true. Pete did understand. And he was right, of course. It was high time she braved the world again. After all, nothing worse could happen to her than had happened in the past.

She bathed and dressed in a black dinner suit with a long narrow skirt, a backless bodice, and a short gold jacket. As usual, she wore her pale hair brushed severely back. She touched up her mouth and applied perfume behind her ears, at her temples, on her throat.

When the downstairs bell rang, she released the catch, reached for her long gloves, evening bag and fur cape. She heard Pete coming up the stairs, two at a time. She opened the door and he stood gaping at her.

"My God, you're stunning, Janet!" He put his arms around her and kissed her cheek. Unexpectedly his mouth found hers, pressed hard, demandingly.

She released herself, a little breathless, color staining her cheeks. "Good heavens! Such — enthusiasm."

He gave her an odd look, a tall, thin man with unruly hair that was nearly flaxen and a hatchet-sharp profile. He almost vibrated with nervous energy.

"Enthusiasm. Well, that's one name for it, of course. I could suggest some others." As she handed him her cape without comment he put it over her shoulders. He grinned. "No curiosity? You don't want to know what they are?"

He shoved a small transparent box into her hand. "Somewhat battered by my — enthusiasm. Hope they'll do."

She fastened the two gardenias to her cape, assuring him that they were lovely. She took her time, unprepared yet to meet his eyes. She should have expected it, of course. The trouble was that she had taken Pete for granted, his steady support, his unvarying good humor, his cheerful devotion. True, she had never taken seriously his love for her. He was, she had always thought, a confirmed bachelor who preferred playing the field to settling down with one woman. But now she wasn't so sure.

She didn't, she told herself firmly, intend

to marry anyone while Cass was incarcerated at Wentworth, but if Pete were to insist on her making a decision, if he were to withdraw his companionship, as he had every right to do, she would be lost without him.

He had been watching the changing play of expression on her face. Now he cocked an eyebrow, half humorously, half ruefully.

"Russlin got carried away. Shall we go sedately to dinner? Oh, I almost forgot. Picked up a little gadget for your kitchenette, cuts sandwiches in different shapes — you just turn this thing."

She laughed as she dropped it on a table. "You and your gadgets! I half expected the gardenias to turn different colors or to burst into song."

He locked the door behind her and followed her down the two flights of stairs to the street. Proudly he displayed the way in which he had fixed up his battered old station wagon. It was equipped for hunting trips, for sleeping, and filled with preposterous gadgets. He drove off in a torrent of words.

He was, she thought, rather magnificent. His defense of Cass had hurt him professionally. Though he worked hard he had not recuperated from the reputation for unscrupulous slickness that had followed the Frederick murder case. And now, any mention of him in the press was apt to carry a string, an innuendo. For all his furious energy he barely managed to make ends meet.

It was easier than Janet had expected to walk into the brilliantly lighted restaurant. There was only one bad moment at the entrance when she braced herself. Then Pete's hand was on her arm, firm and reassuring, and she followed the waiter, walking with head erect, eyes straight ahead.

Over dinner, Pete was at his gayest and she found herself responding to his absurd jokes, relaxed and laughing. When she dared look around she realized that though she had been recognized and though she was being regarded with inevitable curiosity, there was no hostility. Her self-confidence came flooding back. What, after all, had she been afraid of?

Over coffee and brandy, Pete said, "Where do you want to dance?"

She shook her head. "Not tonight, Pete, please."

"Tonight definitely. You're sensationally lovely and I want to show you off."

"Another time. Tonight — I want to do something else." Seeing his face fall she added, "I want you to go with me, if you will."

"Anywhere," he said promptly, as she had known he would.

"I want to go back to the house," she said,

"and I'm a little afraid to go alone."

"The house? You mean Sixty-eighth Street?" He was startled.

She nodded. Unexpectedly she shivered. His hand covered hers, warm and comforting.

"Okay. Then we'll go." He did not speak again until they were in his station wagon. "What is it, dear, a kind of pilgrimage?"

She took a long breath. "I'm going to reopen the house, Pete. I'm going to live there."

His disapproval was heavy in the air though he made no comment until he had turned onto Fifth Avenue and started north. "Won't it be rather steep to keep up?"

"Thornton has agreed to turn over my money."

He whistled. "Well, I'll be damned! What got into him? A change of heart?"

"Blackmail," she said briefly.

He gave her a quick, startled look and made no comment, turned east and pulled in at the curb. In silence they looked at the two identical buildings, four stories in height, each with an areaway and a basement. They had been built by Janet's grandmother when the younger son, Janet's father, married. Twin houses, one for the parents and one for the young couple. When they had been built, the drawing rooms on the first floor had opened into each other and the houses were also joined

41

by a door on the third floor.

After the death of her possessive mother-in-law, Janet's mother had had the other house sealed off and rented. She wasn't, she declared firmly, going to make her son live next door to her when he married.

Actually, Cass and his young wife were to spend the six brief months of their married life in his father's house, but no one had foreseen that then.

Janet sat unmoving in the car while Pete smoked and waited. At last, she drew a long breath. "Well, let's go."

He did not stir. "Why are you doing this, Janet? Hurting yourself. Bringing it all back. You can't live your life with shadows."

"But that's just it!" she said eagerly. "I want to get rid of the shadows and I don't know how else to do it. There are ghosts in this house and I want to exorcise them. With your help. Pete, I want to get hold of that Swiss psychiatrist, Dr. Beldner. He's supposed to be the top man in his field; I want him to come to America, I want him to examine Cass. With his unquestioned reputation, if he were to find Cass sane, as I know he is —"

The girl turned, caught Pete's bony hand between both of hers, pressing it feverishly. The street lights shone on her face, on the enormous dark eyes, making them seem curiously blind.

"I wanted to send for him in the first place. You know that. He could have saved Cass."

"No," Pete said gently. "He could have proved him sane. That wouldn't have saved him. Do you know how many so-called experts I sounded out before I could get men to testify the way I wanted as to Cass's mental condition?"

"I know. You did the only possible thing to help him escape the chair. Without you," her voice broke, "your faith, the way you worked — no one else could have saved him. But now —"

"Well?"

"He's been in Wentworth for three years. He can't be put in jeopardy again for Maitland Frederick's murder. Pete, I want Dr. Beldner to come here. I want him to examine Cass. I want him free. Because he's sane, Pete. You know that. He's sane."

"Yes," Pete said heavily, "he's sane. Of course, you know that it would cost a mint."

"I'll have the money when I need it," she said confidently. "Shall we go in and look at the house?"

"Do you have a key?"

"I telephoned the caretaker. He'll let us in."

The doorbell rang four times without

43

response. Pete ran down the areaway steps and banged on the knocker. A bolt was shot back and the door opened a few inches on a chain.

"Oh, it's you, Mr. Russlin. Miss Grant with you?"

"Yes. Were you asleep?"

"I just wanted to make sure. What with one thing and another going on around here, I don't take any chances. Just a jiffy and I'll have the front door open."

Pete went back to Janet. He was grinning. "What a watchdog you picked! Bolts and chains. Locked up like a safe."

The door opened and Marker, a thin middle-aged man with a balding head, stood back, thrusting an arm into his jacket.

"It's not locked up tight enough," he said, nettled by Pete's comment. "Someone keeps breaking into this place."

"What's that?" Pete was startled. "Why haven't you done anything about it?"

"I reported it to Mr. Grant, Mr. Thornton Grant. I reported it to the police. I got all new locks and put on those bolts and chains. The windows are fastened up as tight as a drum, with those burglar-proof locks. But it don't make any difference. He keeps getting in."

In response to Pete's questions he said, no,

nothing had been taken so far as he could tell, but whoever it was had searched the house, over and over again, from top to bottom, rugs moved, carpets taken up, a regular inch-by-inch search. Especially the rooms on the third floor where Mr. Cass and his wife had lived. Started maybe two months, six weeks ago.

"Got so," Marker said, "I took two looks at my own shadow. And there's creaking and footsteps, but nobody I can see. I'm not a nervous man as a rule but this thing is getting me."

"That," Pete said, "settles it. You aren't going to move back here, Janet. Do you hear me?"

She did not seem to be aware of him. She stood quite still in the circular entrance hall, looking around her. He touched her arm and she started.

"Sorry. I was just remembering. It's all just the same, isn't it?" Her voice was hushed as though she feared to awaken something that slept in the house.

"Just the same." His voice was big and assured. "Same marble floor, same taupe velvet draperies, same crack in that ormolu clock, same red carpet on the stairs. I can remember you coming down those stairs like a whirlwind. I used to be afraid you'd break your neck. And Eve —" He broke off in chagrin at his tactlessness.

"It's all right," she said coolly. "There's no reason why we shouldn't speak of her. After all, this house is full of her."

She remembered standing on the stairs when the front door had opened and Cass came in, looking exultant and scared at the same time. And beside him was a small and smiling girl in a flaming red suit, no hat on her dark hair, white flowers pinned on her jacket.

"Janet," Cass had called, "look what I've brought home for keeps. This is Eve, my wife."

She was, Janet thought, the loveliest creature she had ever seen. She was very young, not more than eighteen, with dark hair and eyes, exquisitely modeled features. But how can you describe beauty? She was one of the world's beautiful women but it was difficult to pick out the small details that made her so, that turned prettiness to breath-taking loveliness.

Eve smiled at Janet and then she came running across the marble floor, holding out both her hands.

"Oh, Janet, I do hope you'll try to like me! I want you to so much."

The gesture, so young, so spontaneous, had been irresistible. It had almost, but not quite, distracted Janet's attention from the young Eve's quick appraising look around her.

From the beginning, Janet told herself, she had tried hard. She had been kind to Eve. She had attempted to conceal the bitterness of her father, who had blamed his daughter-in-law unjustly for his wife's death. She had taught her how to dress and guided her tactfully through her first social encounters, careful not to criticize or to hurt her feelings.

Eve had learned fast. In those few months she had acquired poise and assurance. No, Janet corrected herself, Eve always had assurance. With her arresting kind of beauty she could not help having assurance. And Cass had adored her. He could not take his eyes off her. Cass, spoiled playboy that he had been, thought only of Eve. When his father had clamped down on his allowance and said that if he was old enough to marry he was old enough to support a wife, he had got a job as an automobile salesman, but they had continued to live at home so that Eve could have every comfort.

Not that she was accustomed to it. She never got over her frank delight in the style of living of the Grants, over her childlike pleasure in luxury, over her appreciation of constant and unobtrusive service. She never talked of her family or her background. She had a mother

47

somewhere and a stepfather who seemed to be a helpless invalid. She had been christened Allie Voss. She had, Janet came to suspect, been floating around the fringes of nightclub society when she met Pete. They had a couple of dates — Pete always had a flock of girls on the string — and she had met Cass through him. A week later, they were married. There was little the Grants ever knew about her except that she loved flowers and excitement and admiration, and that she was an awful coward.

She was also, in an intangible way that Janet could not analyze, somehow pathetic, as though she were a will-less creature, molded by other people; even her beauty was in a way a curious liability.

A few weeks after the marriage, Maitland Frederick took a long lease on the twin house next door. The two houses shared a garden at the back. At the rear of the property there was an old coach house. That, Frederick declared exuberantly, was the irresistible attraction. He wanted to turn it into a studio. His regular studio on 57th Street, he complained, was becoming more and more like Grand Central Station, with friends dropping in at all hours and interrupting his work.

The Grants had made no objection. Maitland Frederick was one of America's finest

48

painters and they were delighted to have the old coach house turned to such good use. There was an advantage, too, in having congenial neighbors, since the garden was shared by both houses, and the Grants had known Mrs. Frederick all her life, her family being as prominent in old New York society as their own.

Looking back now, Janet wondered if there had been any signs they had failed to recognize of the relationship between Frederick and Eve. He was a heavy-set man of fifty, with a dissipated face but immense vitality and vaunted virility. Now and then, rumors were heard about the parties he gave in his 57th Street studio, parties which Mrs. Frederick did not attend. Though women seemed to find the man irresistible, Janet had never liked him. Eve had appeared to pay no particular attention to him, beyond demanding a normal tribute to her beauty.

It was only a month before the murder that Janet became aware that her sister-in-law was involved with another man. Little things at first. Eve's new habit of slipping downstairs early in the morning to go through the mail that was left on the long table in the foyer until it could be distributed. Eve who loved to have a late and leisurely breakfast tray while she wore one of her dainty and extravagant bed jackets. The telephone calls made in hurried whispers or broken off when anyone passed. Her disappearance for hours on end, which she accounted for vaguely as shopping, though no packages were delivered; or calling on old friends, though none ever appeared at the 68th Street house.

The last three days before the murder, Eve had been nervous and distraught. Her eyes were swollen as though she had been crying. On the morning of the murder Janet heard her saying hysterically, "I can't find it anywhere! It's gone, I tell you. O God, if anyone else finds it —"

She had become aware of Janet then, whispered, "The telephone," and stopped talking.

Janet put her hands over her eyes, as though she could shut out the memories that had assailed her the minute she entered the house. Pete, who had been watching her, said quietly, "Had enough? Let's go."

"No, I want to look through the house and I'd rather have you with me. It should be in good shape. I'll hire a staff right away. Come along."

She went swiftly through the big formal drawing room, its furniture and paintings muffled in dust covers, the large tapestry on one wall that covered the place where the wall between the drawing room and that in the other house had been sealed over; through the library, with its low couches and book-lined walls, and her mother's small morning room, with the French doors that opened onto the garden. Across the hall were the music room, stiff and formal, with gilt chairs against the walls; dining room, small breakfast room, and kitchen.

Pete followed her upstairs. The bedrooms and dressing rooms of her father and mother were on the left; Cass's room, a guest room and her bedroom on the right of the second floor.

She paused for a moment at the door of her old room. In another life, it seemed to her, she had redecorated it in gold and copenhagen blue, with a flaming red pouf before the dressing table. Just before the murder. A lifetime away. This room had belonged to another person, the popular society girl whose name and picture appeared week after week in the social columns of the *Herald-Tribune*. It did not belong to Katherine Lord, struggling young dress designer.

She went to the window to look out onto the back of the house, trying to peer down into the garden toward the studio where Maitland Frederick had been strangled to death. But the darkness was unrelieved by a single light.

"That's where it happened," she said un-necessarily.

Pete started to protest, saw her expression, and changed his mind. He followed her up to the third floor. The rooms that Cass and Eve had shared after their marriage were on the back overlooking the garden and directly over Janet's room. The servants' rooms were on the front of the house.

"Let's go downstairs, Janet. Suppose you tell me what you remember."

"We went through all that before the trail. Over and over."

"Tell me again. Get it out of your system before it becomes an obsession with you."

She let Pete take her down to the library, where he pulled the cover off a sofa and pushed her gently back against the cushions. He went down to the basement in search of the caretaker and came back with an armload of wood for the fireplace. He was followed by Marker, carrying a tray with bottles, glasses and ice.

Pete built up a fire, mixed drinks and put one in her hand. "Now then." He put an arm around her with impersonal affection and she rested her head against his shoulder.

"How good you are!"

He grinned. "That's almost as bad as being called well-meaning. All right, honey. Let's get it off your mind."

"It started when Mrs. Frederick talked to me on the phone. She'd been trying to reach Cass but he had been out all that day with a prospect . . ."

FOUR

"I don't know where Cass is, Mrs. Frederick," Janet said, surprised by the distraught voice of the older woman. Mrs. Maitland Frederick's unshaken poise was proverbial. "Is anything wrong? May I help?"

There was a little pause. "Something is very wrong, Janet. I hadn't intended discussing it with anyone except Cass. But it's gone so far — perhaps —" There was another pause. "It's Eve," she said at last. "She's having an affair with my husband."

"Mrs. Frederick!"

"She's been meeting him out in the garden studio. I wanted to be sure. When I questioned Maitland he admitted that she had been there a lot. He said he's been —" This time the pause seemed interminable. "He said he's been painting her. She's so fantastically beautiful, of course, I thought I'd been wrong. But this morning, while Maitland was down at his Fifty-seventh Street place, I went out to the studio. I saw the painting he's been doing."

Janet made no reply. Her hand seemed to have frozen on the telephone.

"I have shut my eyes to Maitland's infidelities in the past," Mrs. Frederick went on.

54

"But this, and practically in my own house — no. As I can't reach Cass, you'll have to do it. Tell him to keep his wife away from here. If she ever comes inside the house again I'll divorce Maitland and I'll name Eve. That compromising picture is all the evidence I'll need."

Janet set the telephone down blindly. Mrs. Frederick was going through a trying time of life. Sometimes women got queer, imagined things. But she hadn't sounded mad, only horribly shocked and upset. And determined. She meant every word of it.

Janet shrank away from the thought of a possible scandal. Her father would hit the roof. The Grant temper would explode. And Cass? Poor Cass!

She went slowly, reluctantly, up the stairs to the third-floor suite of rooms where Cass and Eve lived. As usual, it was cluttered with all the paraphernalia that Eve simply dropped wherever she happened to be. How on earth had she managed before she had servants to clean up after her? As usual, too, the suite was filled with the flowers that she loved.

Eve herself was in a corner of a couch doing her nails and watching the television screen. She wore a blue cotton playsuit, her slim brown legs curled up under her, and she looked about fourteen. For a moment Janet felt an upsurge of hope. It couldn't be true. It simply couldn't be true. Not this exquisite child with the wide innocent eyes.

"Hi, Janet. How do you like this new polish?"

"It's too dark," Janet answered automatically. The only ugly thing about Eve were her hands, thick and clumsy, with broad thumbs that curled backward. "You need a lighter, less conspicuous shade."

Eve turned her hand thoughtfully and nodded. "I wish I had your flair, Janet. I can't tell when things look right." As Janet switched off the television program she protested. "Hey, I want to see the rest of that show. He's kind of cute."

"I've got to talk to you," Janet said.

Hearing the strained note in her sister-in-law's voice, Eve had stiffened, she seemed to gather herself together on the couch. She was always afraid of things. Janet wondered fleetingly what kind of life the girl had led in the past, what had frightened her. But there was no time for that now.

"Something pretty unpleasant has happened, Eve. I just had a telephone call from Mrs. Frederick. She has been trying to reach Cass all day. When she couldn't find him —"

Janet saw the trapped look in Eve's eyes and knew in a flash that it was true. She repeated the woman's words of warning.

"No!" Eve cried. "Oh, no! It's not so. I wouldn't do a thing like that. Mait — he's just doing a portrait, a surprise for Cass. That's all there is to it. I swear it is."

"Then what are you afraid of?"

Eve shrank from the coldness in Janet's voice. "Cass," she whispered. "He'll be so angry."

"He'd never be angry with you. He's crazy about you."

"I know," Eve said frankly. "But he might do something impulsive. Don't tell him, Janet. Please."

"I'll have to. If I don't tell him, Mrs. Frederick will. She means business. Unless, of course, you'd rather do it yourself."

"Oh, no, I couldn't. Only please don't let her get a divorce. Don't let her make your father angry. Make me lose all this." She added quickly, "Lose Cass."

Janet went out of the room without reply. She heard Eve wail, "Janet, come back; I've got to talk to you." For a moment she hesitated and then she went on toward the stairs. From the room behind her she heard Eve dialing a telephone number.

A half hour later Cass had come home. Thornton was with him. They had met by chance on the street outside the house. Thornton, it appeared, had come to call on Janet's father, who was shut up in his room with a bout of influenza.

While Thornton waited in the library for the butler to announce him, sipping dry sherry and looking at some new acquisitions which had not yet been catalogued, Janet pulled Cass into the music room across the hall, closed the door and told him about Mrs. Frederick's call. She watched the hot rage rise in his face. He lunged toward the door and she ran to catch his arm.

"Wait, Cass! Before you do anything you'd be sorry for, talk to Eve."

"I'm not going to involve her."

"She knows already. If you quarrel with the Fredericks, she'll be publicly involved."

Cass hesitated, uncertain as to what to do. Then he left the room, running up the stairs to the third floor. Janet clenched her fists and then went in search of Thornton. She poured out her story incoherently. "Cass is with Eve now," she concluded, "but he's feeling murderous. You've got to get over to the Fredericks' before he does. You've got to find a way to handle this thing and prevent a scandal."

As he stared at her she caught him by the shoulder and pushed him toward the door. "Hurry! We don't want some awful scene.

After all, it may be a mistake."

"But of course it's a mistake." With maddening deliberation Thornton smoothed his hair, straightened his tie, pulled down his cuffs before he let himself out. A few minutes later Janet heard Cass clattering down the stairs, heard the crash of the front door as he slammed it behind him.

She ran up the stairs to her own room and opened the window to lean far out. Over the hedges she could see the studio at the back. A window cleaner in white overalls, with a white cap on his head, was perched on a ladder but he wasn't working. He was staring, transfixed, through the skylight. Slowly he backed down, moving with an awkward lurch.

Janet waited, her heart thumping. Then she saw the white cap moving along between the high hedges. There was no sign of Cass. How long would he go on talking to Frederick? Please God, don't let them fight!

She closed the window, embarrassed at being caught spying on the studio, but the step that startled her was not in her room. It was overhead, a curious halting step. Then she heard Eve give a sharp cry, which was broken off as though a hand had been shoved over her mouth.

The fire in the library had burned down

59

and Pete got up to replenish it. He gathered up the two glasses and replenished them, too. Without his comforting arm around her, Janet felt chilly. She slipped on her fur jacket.

Pete thrust the tall glass into her hand and went to stand by the fireplace, looking down at her, a troubled expression on his face.

"And that's all you know? Of your own observation, I mean."

She nodded.

"You didn't see Cass when he went out to the coach house or when he came back?"

She shook her head.

"Or anyone else?"

Another shake.

"So there we are, back to the limping man, the window cleaner whom no one hired, the window cleaner whom no one but you ever saw."

"Eve saw him. He came into this house. He went up to her room. He struck her. That's when she cried out. He's the one who bruised her face like that. Not Cass! Never Cass. And yet half the prosecution's case was based on the bruise she had at the time of the murder, evidence that Cass had believed her to be guilty, a visible proof of his violence. That's why I could never forgive Eve. She could have saved Cass. I knew it then and I know it now."

"God knows I did everything a man could

60

do to unearth that limping window cleaner. And so did the police. But he vanished into thin air."

"That's all you ever thought he was, Pete. I always knew that. You played along with me because you thought I was making a desperate effort to help Cass by producing a red herring. But a window cleaner who limps! I could have done better than that. He was real. I told you the truth. He followed me for weeks before the trial. I didn't imagine that. And today I heard him again! I couldn't mistake the peculiar rhythm of that halting step."

Pete gave her a quick look, alerted by the rising pitch of her voice. "Who did you think he was?" he asked, his voice so big and matter-of-fact he might have been ordering a meal. "The real murderer?"

She shook her head. "That doesn't make sense. But certainly he saw the murder done."

"And he knew Eve?"

"Well enough to hit her."

Unexpectedly Pete chuckled. "You really hate her, don't you, Janet?"

"That's what Thornton told me today. I don't think so. Hatred's an ugly thing, a destructive thing. I don't like her. I never liked her. Not because she was such a common little thing; if she had been a good wife to Cass and made him happy that wouldn't have

61

mattered a scrap. But she was on the make; it kept creeping through what she said when she was off-guard. She didn't care a scrap for Cass; she used him as she used us all. And after the trial, of course, she never went near him. She never visited him a single time. She got her divorce as fast as she could."

"Did you ever know anything about her family?"

"She certainly never brought any of them here, though we urged her to. Whatever they were like we'd have made them welcome. She never talked about the past. She might have been born the day she walked into the house with Cass, looking like the cat that swallowed the canary. Her real name was Allie Voss. I knew that because she had to put it on the marriage license. Eve seems to have been her own idea."

"Should have been Lilith," Pete commented.

"She has a mother somewhere and a stepfather, but I always understood that they lived in the South because of his health."

"I remember they didn't show up at the trial."

"How did you meet Eve, Pete?"

"She was with a group of people at a nightclub somewhere. I knew one of the men the way you do people you just nod to. The guy

Eve was with got loaded and they had to ease him out. Fellow I knew called me over to even up the numbers. I danced with Eve and took her home. Then we had a couple of dates. And then we ran into Cass at a bar. After that," Pete gave her an apologetic smile, "conflagration. Cass went down for the count, if I may mix the metaphor."

"You're not to blame," she said gently. She squared her shoulders. "Just the same, the time has come to get Cass out of Wentworth." When Pete made no reply she looked up at him in surprise. "You know he's sane."

"You just aren't thinking, dear. You don't realize —"

"You don't realize," she interrupted, "what it's like for Cass in Wentworth."

He shook his head. "You don't realize what it would be like for Cass to be out of Wentworth. Wherever he went, every day of his life, he'd be the murderer of Maitland Frederick."

The brightness died out of Janet's face. Pete saw her stricken expression and came back to put both arms around her, rocking her gently, his cheek pressed against her hair.

"You've forgotten how it was, how bitter the press was when he escaped the chair, the howl that went up when I pulled every string there was to get him out of the state asylum and into Wentworth. You've forgotten how much feeling was excited by the murder of America's most prominent painter. There is no question in people's minds about Cass's guilt. He went over to the Frederick house to have things out. He was inside that studio for fifteen minutes. When he came out Frederick was dead, strangled."

"Cass found him dead."

"Then what was he doing in there?"

"I don't know," Janet said desperately. "I've always thought he was destroying that painting of Eve. After all, a burned canvas was found in the fireplace."

"Then why did he deny there was such a painting? Why did Mrs. Frederick deny it on the stand, under oath?"

"I don't know why, but I'm sure she saw it. Cass wanted to protect Eve from scandal."

"Murder was no way to protect her from that."

"Pete, suppose, just suppose, Cass didn't lie. Suppose Maitland Frederick was dead when he got there."

"But, darling, there was no one else. No opportunity. No motive."

"So all the time," she said slowly, "you've really believed that Cass was guilty."

Pete took both her hands, his narrow face without its usual look of amusement, stripped of everything but the intensity of his feeling.

"I always knew he was guilty but I did my damnedest for him. You've got to believe that. God knows I did! And I'd do it again. Don't misunderstand me. Cass was — is my best friend. And Eve is — no wonder she drove him crazy. She's an evil woman. But," he held her eyes, "leave Cass where he is, Janet my darling. He is safe there. For God's sake, let's not crowd our luck."

Janet's hands clung to his, feeling as always their warmth and assurance. "You all say that: Mrs. Frederick and Thornton and now you. But it's no good, Pete. We Grants never give up. I'll never believe Cass is dangerous and," her voice hardened, "I'll never believe he was guilty of murder."

Pete tried to release the tension in her tired, white face. "And to what, Miss Grant," he said lightly, "do you attribute the murder of Maitland Frederick? The gremlins?"

"Mrs. Frederick had been in the studio," she said stubbornly.

Pete forced a grin. "She could hardly have managed to kill a big active man like her husband."

"And Thornton was there. Thornton's story was that he had gone out to the studio, knocked and got no answer, but he heard someone moving around inside. He assumed that, for some reason, Frederick didn't want to admit him. But suppose it was the murderer he heard in the studio. Or — suppose he lied."

"But why in God's name would Thornton have killed Frederick?"

"I don't know," she admitted. Her expression changed.

"What is it?" he asked quietly, watching her.

"Pete, do you think that Thornton was in love with Eve, too? That he was carrying on an affair with her?"

His effort to swallow his laugh made her smile in spite of her dead earnestness.

"I know how absurd it sounds. Thornton is so — impeccable. But if Eve had one lover, she might have had more."

"You seem to be sure she was unfaithful. Rather late in the day, isn't it, to come to that conclusion?"

"I knew it for weeks before the murder by the way she acted."

"And you never told me."

"I couldn't, before the trial. I provided Cass with a motive and I was afraid. So afraid."

He held her cold hand and chafed it gently. "You've been brooding too long, living too much in the past. Break away from it, Janet. Sell the damned house. Exorcise the ghosts."

"And what about the person who has been

searching this place? What about him?"

Pete grinned. "What do you think he's been looking for? The jools? The Secret Papers?"

"Eve's letters," she surprised him by saying. "She hid them."

He gave a startled ejaculation. "Are you guessing again?"

"No, I heard her on the telephone. She was frantic."

"You think they are still somewhere in this house?"

"They could be. She was always sloppy and careless. She mislaid them and can't remember what she did with them. I'm going to find them if they are here, Pete."

"Okay, gal. More power to you." He pulled her to her feet. "Now I'm going to take you home. You look like hell."

She laughed. "Always the diplomat. Anyhow, I want to go home. Tonight, I'm going to write to Dr. Beldner."

FIVE

On a January night black headlines screamed from the newsstands: *Cass Grant Declared Sane. Frederick Murderer Released. Sister Frees Playboy Killer.*

At the wheel of the car that had brought them down from Wentworth, Pete Russlin cursed softly and monotonously to himself after he caught sight of the newspapers. Janet, seated beside Cass in back, protested sharply on a note of pain, "Oh, no!" Cass said nothing at all, but as he leaned forward to press out his cigarette in the ashtray, street lights touched his prematurely white hair, the grim lines in his face, the curious intentness of his eyes.

He was, Janet thought, a man of purpose if she had ever seen one and she wished to heaven she could guess at his purpose. Only once in the three months since she had begun the fight for his release had he made any comment.

"What do you plan to do — afterwards?" she had said tentatively.

He had given her an odd look. "I have some unfinished business." He had never amplified the statement.

68

Even with fur-lined gloves her hands were cold, though the car heater was functioning smoothly. What had brought that look to Cass's face? What did he intend to do?

Never once, since the day of the murder, had he mentioned Eve's name to her, had he referred to her even obliquely, Eve whom he had adored. For a clear moment Janet thought that this was what Pete had been afraid of, and then denied the existence of the thought. Never, she told herself firmly, had she doubted Cass. Never for a moment.

As the car turned into Fifth Avenue Cass's eyebrows lifted. "What the hell?"

"I've reopened the house."

"Aren't you doing this the hard way, Jan!"

"That's what I told her," Pete put in.

"There isn't any other way," she said. "Anyhow, Mrs. Frederick gave up her lease. The other house is empty. Do you mind very much!"

"What difference does it make?" Cass gave a mirthless chuckle. "The playboy killer!"

The car jerked as Pete slammed on the brake. "God damn all ghouls! The dirty — let's not stop here, Janet. We'll go on to my place."

Outside the twin houses a crowd had gathered, some of them newsmen and photographers, most of them curiosity seekers. A

69

policeman was saying monotonously, "Keep moving. Keep moving." A prowl car slid in at the curb.

"No," Cass said, "it has to be faced sometime. Let's get it over with."

Pete hesitated, ignoring the impatient horn of the car behind him.

Janet took a long breath. She had asked for this. "Cass is right. We've got to see it through now."

One of the men in the prowl car got out to wave them on. Pete spoke quietly and, after a quick look, the officer nodded. The car parked at the curb and Cass, his face set, got out and held his hand to Janet. The crowd moved closer. Pete was on Janet's other side now and the three turned, helpless and trapped, to face the battery of cameras.

A clamor of voices rose. "How does it feel to be free, Mr. Grant? . . . What are your plans? . . . Is it true that you are going to attend your ex-wife's opening night?"

Pete said shortly, "No comment," and used his shoulders to form a shield for Janet, to get her through the crowd to the front door. Cass followed, hard eyes on the newsmen, on the crowd that stared, on the watchful police. The door was opened by the new butler whom Janet had hired and then it closed behind them, shutting out the inquisitive eyes, the impertinent voices.

Cass looked around him, his face impassive. Only when he handed the butler his hat and coat did Janet see that his hands were shaking.

"You're in your old room on the second floor," she said. "We'll have cocktails in the library, Howell. Pete, you're staying for dinner, aren't you? We aren't going to change tonight." As he hesitated she added quickly, "Cass and I were counting on you."

Pete answered the appeal in her voice. "Glad to. Like old times."

He sounded too hearty as Janet had sounded too eager. For some reason they couldn't be natural, couldn't break through this new restraint. Cass looked from one to the other, a sardonic twist to his mouth. Then he went quickly up the stairs.

Later, while Pete threw another log on the fire in the library, Cass mixed and passed martinis, and settled himself in a deep chair, the forgotten glass in his hand, eyes far away, brooding. Janet stole a look at him but he was unaware of her, sunk in dark thoughts of his own. How changed he was. How remote. As far from her now as he had been at Wentworth, and as unreachable.

Pete lifted his glass. "What shall we drink to? The future?"

"Together again," Janet suggested.

71

"Unfinished business," Cass said.

Pete set down his untasted drink. "Look here, Cass, the past is the past. Forget it. Don't be a fool."

"Take it easy, Pete. I don't want any legal advice tonight. We're celebrating. Remember? The Frederick murderer has been restored to his happy home."

There was a crash and a tinkle of glass. Shortly afterwards Howell came in. "Someone threw a stone at one of the drawing room windows. I've called the police. There won't be any further disturbance tonight."

For the first time since his release, Cass laughed aloud.

At Cass's insistence they had coffee in the drawing room, the draperies closed tight. The hole in the window pane had been temporarily stopped and the glass fragments removed. Outside the house a policeman paced up and down. The crowds had gone. Fortunately, it was a bitter night, snow whipped almost into a blizzard by the sharp gusty wind. At least, it would discourage loiterers.

Howell came into the room. "Mr. Grant," he announced.

Thornton paused for a moment in the doorway. "Good evening, Janet. I thought you'd be here, Russlin. Well, Cass." He came forward with outstretched hand, his lips barely moving in a small tight smile.

Cass shook hands. "Come to welcome the prodigal?"

Thornton accepted coffee and refused brandy. After a moment's uncomfortable lull he offered the opinion that it was a cold night. They agreed. Seasonable, though. Again they acquiesced. Of course, you had to expect some cold weather this time of year. No one disputed the point. January was the month for Florida, all right, or the Virgin Islands. Maybe even South America. Summer down there. Blazing hot sunshine right now. Hard to realize, wasn't it?

Cass stirred, looked at his older cousin, his brows raised, making deep wrinkles in his forehead. "What the hell are you leading up to, Thornton?"

Thornton gave a dry little cough. "You've seen the papers?"

"We saw the headlines. They were enough."

"Why don't you go away, Cass? You won't be able to live here. Aside from the fact that it isn't fair to Janet —"

"Suppose," Janet began hotly.

Thornton put up his hand, pearl cuff links catching the light momentarily. "And not fair to you either, Cass. There's no possible life

73

for you here. But you're still young, only thirty-three. Go away. Start over. Build yourself a new life from scratch. Now if you were to change your name —"

"I have no intention of changing my name," Cass said coolly. "I intend to clear it."

Thornton finished his coffee, set down the small cup with his usual deliberation. "And yet Dr. Beldner actually helped you get out of Wentworth," he said in a tone of wonder.

O God, Janet prayed, don't let Cass lose his temper. But Cass, she saw in relief, was smiling.

"Don't get any ideas, Thornton," he said gently. "I'm not going back there."

"My dear fellow," Thornton never knew how to address people with the proper tone of bonhomie, "you aren't aware of the situation. The mud has settled. Don't stir it up again."

"But the mud is still there," Cass pointed out. "I want to clear the waters."

"What, exactly, do you intend to do?"

"For four years I've been thinking about one thing: Who really killed Maitland Frederick? The police were so happy with the case against me that they never, so far as I could make out, looked for anyone else. There I was, made to order. I intend to find the man you heard prowling around in Frederick's studio

74

before I went in."

"That was Frederick himself. It must have been."

Cass leaned forward "How do you know that, Thornton?"

Thornton made an abrupt, uncharacteristic gesture of exasperation. He turned to Pete who had been listening intently, who had not said a word, his clever profile as sharp as a knife blade. "Can't you lay it on the line for him, Russlin? Point out he'd better stop while he's still ahead?"

"You know they can't try me again for Frederick's murder," Cass pointed out.

"But even if you don't care what you do to Janet, to the family name, to me, have you thought about Eve?"

"Not when I could help it," Cass said, his lips white.

"Don't rake up more trouble and notoriety for her, Cass." Thornton was in dead earnest. "She's made a new start. An actress. She's opening this week in a starring role. A Graham Collinge play, and you know what that means in the way of prestige. She's built a new life. She's going to remarry."

"God help the poor devil," Cass said.

Howell was in the doorway again, looking distressed. Before he could speak a woman had brushed past him. A small woman with dark hair, a long ermine coat with orchids fastened to it by a diamond pin. An exquisitely beautiful woman. Eve.

For a moment there wasn't a sound in the room. No one seemed to breathe. Then the three men got to their feet.

Eve looked from face to face. She's frightened, Janet thought in surprise. She's always been an awful coward. But, then, what is she doing here?

And then Eve went straight to Cass, her coat swinging open, revealing the sequined pink evening dress, its straps crossed over her breast, and her bare shoulders — what wretched taste the girl had, but what heartbreaking beauty. She stretched out her hands to him in an appealing gesture.

"Cass," she said, "I'm glad you're free. Truly I am. I don't want us to be enemies."

There was no expression on Cass's face. He looked at the girl whom he had profoundly loved, the wife who had left his world in wreckage, and there was nothing to be read.

The outstretched hands dropped to her sides, then gripped each other. "Cass, you loved me once. Be generous with me. I deserve to be happy. I'm so young. And I'm going to be married — if you don't spoil everything."

"Thornton just told us," Pete broke in

harshly. "Nice timing, Eve. Quite a surprise."

Cass said nothing at all.

"Oh." Eve caught her breath. Then she smiled radiantly, went to slip her hand under Thornton's arm. "Then won't you be nice, Cass dear? Won't you give us your good wishes?"

"Thornton! Well, I'll be damned." Cass threw back his head and shouted with laughter.

Color stained Thornton's usually pale cheeks. He's thrown off balance, Janet thought. He didn't want it to happen this way.

He pressed Eve's gloved hand with his own and the look he gave her was one of hopeless infatuation. "You shouldn't have come here, Precious."

Precious! Janet bit her lip to keep from giggling. Thornton, who loathed endearments, had really gone off the deep end.

"I thought," Eve said in her touchingly childish voice, "if Cass just understood, everything would be all right. No misunderstandings between us. You do understand, don't you, Cass darling?"

"Eve," Thornton said in remonstrance.

Janet tried to catch Pete's eye but he had turned his back squarely on the girl who had so nearly sworn away the life of his best friend.

With the toe of his shoe he kicked a log back on the fire.

"Sure," Cass said, his tone amused. "Thornton now has my money as well as his own. What misunderstanding could there possibly be?"

There were flecks of red on the whites of Thornton's eyes and Janet thought in surprise, I never knew before he had the Grant temper.

But Thornton had no intention of losing his temper. He pressed Eve's hand again and said, "Let's go, dearest. There's no reason why you should be subjected to insults." He ignored Cass, addressed the lawyer's back. "Russlin, you had better warn your client. He seems to need legal advice. Eve is not to be persecuted. Is that clear?"

Pete did not turn or speak. Eve looked as though she wanted to intervene, changed her mind. A pulse beat in her cheek, in her throat. For all her beauty she seemed hag-ridden.

She rubbed her cheek caressingly against Thornton's sleeve. "Cass doesn't mean it," she said, "and I want us to be friends. I want so terribly to be friends." She turned to Janet. "Please, Janet, please. All I ask is that you — and Cass — let people see you don't hate me. Is that so much to ask?"

"Eve," Janet said, "I wish you'd tell me

78

what you want and then go. You have no place here anymore."

There were tears in Eve's eyes. She had always been able to cry at the drop of a hat. She wiped them away with a childish gesture. "Don't blame me for what happened, Janet. Be fair."

"You're trembling," Thornton said in concern. "Let me take you home."

"I — may I sit down?"

Thornton put Eve into a chair and looked down at her anxiously. Then he splashed some brandy into a glass and watched her sip it. Under the careful make-up she was ghastly.

"What's wrong?" Janet asked.

"Just nerves," Eve said vaguely. "Things have been upset at the theater. Little things going wrong." As though unwilling to break contact with Janet she added, "How wonderful that color is on you. I don't know anyone else who could wear it. I wish you had designed my costumes for *Fatal Lady*, but, I don't know, I sort of hesitated to ask you."

"Really," Janet said, "you are incredible."

"No, Janet. Don't be angry. Don't be hostile." The tears gushed now. "Please. For everyone's sake. We've all been unhappy. Let's —" A pause. "Let's be friends." She put down the brandy glass, came to kneel be-

79

side Janet's chair.

"Listen to me, Janet. It's just a little thing really. I want you to come to the dress rehearsal tomorrow night."

"Like hell she will!" Cass exploded.

She flung out a hand to silence him, her eyes on Janet, tears spilling unheeded down her cheeks, the tip of her nose turning pink. "If you come, Janet, it will stop all the ugly gossip. It's as bad for you and Cass as it will be for Thorny and me. If you'd think, you'd see that for yourself. Just be there. Then when Thorny and I are married there will he no big fuss." Her eyes met Janet's, she added as though trying to convey a message, "You'll be glad you came. Really you will. I promise."

Pete turned around slowly. "Actually, Eve may be right. One big story in the press and then the whole thing will stop being news."

Eva got to her feet and, with her amazing recuperative powers, powdered her nose and repaired her make-up. She was like a cat stopping in mid-play to wash a paw.

"Then you'll come?" Again it seemed to Janet that she was trying to convey a message.

Pete nodded at Janet who said reluctantly, "All right. I'll come."

"We'll be with you, Janet," Cass told her.

At his expression Eve's face crinkled with alarm and she clutched at Thornton's sleeve.

With a long hostile look from face to face, Thornton took her away.

"Well," Janet said on a long breath. "Eve and Thornton. Thorny! Well! Are you sure that you are right about this, Pete?"

"It's probably the best thing we could do," Pete said slowly.

"I wonder," Cass said, "what she was really after."

SIX

"I wonder," Mr. Potter said thoughtfully, "what you are really after."

Graham Collinge lifted his voice in complaint. He had, at considerable inconvenience to himself, taken in his friend, his so-called friend, given him a shelter while his Gramercy Park house was being redecorated. He had put up with Mr. Potter's curious acquaintances and the newsmen who had come sniffing around the door, scenting out a story.

At this point, he said bitterly, his background was probably being checked by the police simply because by harboring Mr. Potter he became suspect. All this he had endured without complaint. But now, to have his motives impuned, his disinterested friendship doubted, was too much.

"I think," Mr. Potter said in a judicial tone, "that scene would play better if you broke into tears."

The playwright broke into laughter. He was, like Mr. Potter, in his middle thirties. Like him, too, he was slight and fair. Unlike him, he was tall. He had a pleasant ugly face. Considering his success in his field, which had brought with it not only prestige but money, he was reasonably unspoiled and kept his vanity under good control. He had reached the point where adverse criticism surprised and grieved him but it no longer frightened him. He could afford it.

He had been sprawling on a couch in the living room of his penthouse apartment on Central Park South, wearing a pair of loud striped pajamas and a dark silk robe. He got up now to open the draperies, whose modernistic design, Mr. Potter told him, resembled lightning that had been processed by automation. He looked out at the heavily falling snow, shivered, and pulled the draperies together again.

"Speaking of playing scenes," he began casually, "would you care to come along to the dress rehearsal tonight?" He wandered across the room to the bar. "Yours is Haig & Haig, isn't it?" He came back and put the tall glass beside his guest.

Mr. Potter grinned. "For a minute I thought you were going to pat me on the head."

"Damn it," the playwright began, goaded by his friend's amusement, and then he answered the grin. He mixed himself a Bloody Mary and came back to pull up a chair facing Mr. Potter.

The latter raised his glass. "Success to the new play. But why *Fatal Lady*? Isn't melodrama a departure for you?"

Collinge nodded. "A kind of reaction. My plays were getting so way-out I didn't understand them myself, and I wanted to see if I could put together an old-fashioned play with a strong situation and a firm plot line. It won't help my reputation but it has been rather fun."

"And why Eve Grant?"

"Because," Collinge said frankly, "she is the most beautiful creature on earth. She'll pack in the customers."

"Can she act?"

Collinge grinned. "Not on the stage," he admitted, "but it isn't necessary. The play follows the main lines of the Frederick murder case and that's all the public will need. Oh, the details have been changed, of course. And the murderer — I've made the victim's wife the real killer. It provides a big scene between the two women. The character actress I've got for the part is one of the best in the business. She's terrific. She can carry the scene for both of them. All Eve has to do is to look beautiful. In fact, that's all she can do."

"You'll be luckier than you deserve," Mr. Potter warned him, "if Mrs. Frederick doesn't clap a libel suit on you."

"Nuts," Collinge said lightly. "No one ever

84

doubted that Cass Grant really killed the man."

"I did," Mr. Potter startled him by saying. "I sat through the whole trial. After all, it was the most sensational murder of the century. Big families. Money. Society. Great painter. Artist's model. Beautiful women."

"But Grant must have killed him! There was no one else, unless you believe in that window cleaner the sister claimed to see."

"She saw something. She was the only one of the lot who wasn't lying." Mr. Potter sipped his drink. "I remember her very clearly. Extraordinary eyes the girl had. Almost black. The other one, Eve, was scared stiff. What was she afraid of? Or whom?" He put down his glass. "Look here, Collinge, you're playing with explosives. Grant was released yesterday. You saw the papers? This thing is stirring up all the old scandal."

"It's too late to call it off now. We open tomorrow night. Anyhow, that's not my trouble." As though he had said too much, Collinge reached out to flick on the television set. "Time for the news."

Mr. Potter gave him a thoughtful look. The set warmed up.

"After three years at Wentworth, where he had been committed as criminally insane, after escaping a first-degree murder verdict by reason of insanity, Cass Grant was released yesterday. Dr. Franz Beldner, world-famous Swiss alienist, examined him intensively and declared him sane. Mr. Grant, reached at his family home on East Sixty-eighth Street, next door to the Frederick house, made the following statement."

The scene switched to the library of the Grant house. Cass Grant stood facing the cameras, speaking quietly. Beside him, Janet watched, standing very erect, very stiff, her eyes on her brother's face.

"Four years ago," Cass said, "Maitland Frederick was murdered in his studio behind this house. I have only one purpose in life, to find his killer and to clear my name. At the time of the trial I swore that I was innocent. Now I am going to prove it."

The picture switched back to the commentator. "Today, the New York traffic problem again engaged . . ."

Collinge snapped off the set. "God," he said aghast, "what happened to Grant up there? He's so old, so changed."

"I was right about that girl's eyes," Mr. Potter said. "They are magnificent."

Collinge gave him an uneasy look. He picked up his glass. "Well," he said defiantly, "it ought to be good publicity."

Mr. Potter leaned forward. "Call off the

play," he said, a note of urgency in his voice, "or lock up your Eve. That man means business." He added smoothly, "Is that why you sent for me?"

Collinge abandoned pretense. "Oh, no. Nothing like that. It's just — little things. Malicious mischief. Someone trying to break Eve's nerve."

"You don't mind?" Collinge asked. "It's just that you are good at things like that." His voice trailed off uncertainly.

Mr. Potter held out his glass for a refill. When he brought it back, Collinge studied his friend. Friend? Hardly that. An acquaintance of several years' standing. That was about all. Mr. Potter had come to him twice in the past because theater people had been involved in murder cases. He couldn't, the playwright admitted to himself, figure Potter out. A man of inherited wealth, he had, for half a dozen years or more, been involved, or had involved himself, with murder. Occasionally his involvement brought him a great deal of newspaper publicity. More often, Collinge suspected, he remained, where he preferred to be, in the background. Not a man to be close to but a man of whom you thought instinctively when you were in trouble.

"That is," Collinge went on awkwardly,

"you're always involving yourself in queer situations."

"Usually murder," Mr. Potter corrected him. "Do I take it that you are expecting violence?"

"Good God, no!" Collinge was genuinely shocked. "Nothing like that. But, Potter, why murder?"

"Because there's no civilization without respect for human life. To the extent that we disregard human life we fail abjectly as human beings."

"But the police —"

"Let me give you some facts, Collinge. Murder rates high as a cause of death in some parts of this country. There is murder done every forty-five minutes. About every two hours there is what might be called a perfect crime. Every two hours! About sixty percent of murderers get of scotfree; free to kill again.

"That situation isn't true just of the United States, of course. A few years ago, a British criminologist declared that eighty percent of English murderers were walking around as free as air; that fifteen percent were in mental institutions. Only five percent were in prison. Why, the guy who steals a woman's handbag takes a bigger risk of imprisonment than a clever murderer at the present stage of western civilization.

"So what are we going to do about it? Say 'tut-tut' and forget it? Hell, no! Somehow we've got to win back a respect for human life or we're unfit to survive. That's why I can't just say 'tut-tut' or 'it doesn't concern me.' By God, it concerns all of us. So when I get a chance to do something about it, I do."

Mr. Potter broke off his tirade. "Well, that's that. But this thing has grown to such monstrous proportions it has gotten under my skin. I have to do something about it. When more individuals can shake off their apathy and act, we'll get somewhere. Believe me, Collinge, every murder strikes at the heart of civilization; it is an attack on all mankind."

"I didn't know," Collinge said slowly, "you felt like that."

"I don't generally make speeches," Mr. Potter admitted. "Well, that's enough about me. Let's have it."

There was nothing you could pin down, Collinge admitted, but little things kept happening. Eve was crazy about flowers, always had masses of them from her admirers. One morning, when she reported for rehearsal, she discovered that someone had poured all the water out of the vases in her dressing room and the flowers had wilted. Once there was a dead mouse in her cold-cream jar. Once a sliver of broken glass turned up in her powder.

Mr. Potter gave a startled ejaculation. "That's not such a trifle."

"You're telling me," Collinge said grimly. "She has been getting more jittery day by day. Forgetting her lines. She says she isn't sleeping because her phone keeps ringing all night. Then she picks it up and no one answers. At the rehearsal yesterday her face was twitching with nerves and she had to be prompted all through the third act."

"Perhaps she is worked up over her ex-husband's release; afraid to have him at large," Mr. Potter suggested.

"No, nothing got out about that until last night's newscasts. This thing has been going on for weeks. Maybe I was wrong to open cold in New York. I should have taken the damned thing on the road to break her in. But it seemed like the best idea at the time. Hell, I knew the reviews would stink, but we've got a nice advance sale here because of my reputation, and the news value of the thing should carry it."

"A bit late now to cope with the problem, isn't it?" Mr. Potter commented.

"The fool girl didn't tell me until yesterday when I blasted her for muffing her lines. Then it all came out."

"Why hadn't she told you before?"

"I don't know. Personally, I think she has a strong suspicion about who is gunning for her and she's scared out of the few wits she has. That's why I wanted you to come along tonight. You're easy to talk to. Get Eve to talk. Find out what she's afraid of. Then I can handle it. Otherwise, as sure as God made little apples, she's going to crack up at the opening."

"Do we eat first," Mr. Potter inquired, "or do we go to the theater unfortified?"

SEVEN

Snow was still falling heavily when they emerged from Sardi's, sidewalks were slippery, taxis crawled past, discharging their passengers before the theaters. The marquee under which Collinge turned was unlighted. He pushed open the door. A shirt-sleeved man with a dead cigar in his mouth and a racing sheet in his hand was sitting on a stool just inside.

"Evening, Mr. Collinge."

The theater was dark except for the stage, which was brightly lighted. The curtain was up, backdrops in place, and stagehands were placing a Victorian sofa of red plush downstage right.

"It looks like a Guthrie McClintic production," Mr. Potter commented.

Collinge grinned in spite of himself.

"What's the sofa for? The rape or the reconciliation?"

"Oh, dry up."

From the balcony the chief electrician bellowed, "Move that spot! I told you before —"

The stage manager, clutching the prompt book, peered into the darkened theater, called, "That you, Graham?" His next words were

92

drowned in a spate of hammering.

"What's that?" Collinge went quickly down the aisle. He called over his shoulder, "Take a seat anywhere. Bit confused right now. I'll come back for you and introduce you to Eve. Okay?" He went on, stopped again. "Oh, you can smoke here, if you like, long as the fireman doesn't catch you." He stood looking up at the stage. "What the hell is that racket?"

"The door upstage center is stuck, so Eve has to squeeze through. It ruins her entrance. The carpenter will have it working smoothly in a minute."

Mr. Potter pulled down a seat in the darkened theater. As his eyes grew adjusted he saw that two other people were seated in the auditorium. Now and then, a cigarette glowed. Once a flashlight shone and was dark again.

Collinge was on the stage now. He yelled a comment to the electrician and a soft light was focused on the sofa and shut off again. He tried the door at the back to make sure it swung open easily and conferred with the harassed stage manager, who was rapidly becoming demented.

A young actor in evening clothes, white tie dangling in his hand, make-up too obvious under the hard light, hurried across the stage, getting in the way of the stagehands who were

93

lifting a framed picture onto the wall over the fireplace.

"Hey, Fischer, get the hell out," Collinge shouted.

"I'm just checking on that cigarette lighter. It hadn't been filled at rehearsal. Simply maddening. Made me feel like a fool. I was ready to scream."

"Darling," called a full-throated contralto, and a ripe-looking woman in a black evening dress came in through the doorway on the left. "I need a beat after Eve's exit in the second act. I've got a topper there and it's lost unless —"

"We've thrashed that out half a dozen times, Millicent," Collinge said wearily.

Millicent Cawling, of course. Mr. Potter remembered her performance in the past and he was cheered.

"But really, Graham!"

"The tempo has to accelerate right up to the end of the scene. Take a beat there and the whole thing drops. Be an angel, dear, and get the hell off the stage." Collinge gave her a light tap on the behind, looked at his watch and inspected the stage. "Where's Eve?"

The character actress shrugged. "Dressing."

"Tell her to get a move on, will you, dear?"

"Not me. She's talking to someone. When

I tried to borrow a cigarette she wouldn't even let me in. That dresser of hers guards her like a dragon."

Mr. Potter's eyes were adjusted to the dimness now. A few rows ahead of him on the left he made out the features of Sanders Newton, Broadway's best-known and most successful angel. Immediately in front of him was Thornton Grant at whom Mr. Potter looked in considerable surprise. Grant, whom he encountered now and then at his club, was the last man he would have expected to find in attendance at a dress rehearsal.

A discreet scent of perfume made Mr. Potter turn around. The woman who had slipped quietly into the seat behind him was Mrs. Maitland Frederick, her beautifully dressed white hair hatless, a sable coat wrapped closely around her. Mr. Potter edged his way farther along the row of seats to a place where he could keep an unobtrusive eye upon her without appearing to turn his head. It seemed more than likely that Collinge was in for a bad half hour when she discovered that he had cast her as her husband's killer.

There was a wave of cold air and then three people came down the aisle, a slim fair-haired girl accompanied by two men, a tall thin man with a narrow face and an air of nervous energy and a shorter man with graying hair and a hard-bitten manner that was oddly familiar. Mr. Potter searched his memory. Where had he seen him before? The taller man was familiar, too; he had heard him speak, a big, confident, relaxed kind of speech. The girl — she turned and he saw the long dark eyes under tilted brows, the shining smooth hair. Janet Grant, of course. Then the hard-bitten man was Cass Grant and the taller one must be Russlin the lawyer.

Collinge had been on and off the stage. Now he dropped off lightly and sat in the front row. The curtains closed.

"All right," he called. "Lights! Curtain!"

The footlights went up and the curtains swirled apart. Fischer, the young man in evening clothes, was pacing across the stage. He paused to check his watch with the clock on the mantel. The door upstage center was flung wide and Eve Grant stood for a moment, arms out, a black evening cape lined with scarlet satin swinging open to reveal a low-cut evening dress. She was incredibly lovely. For a long moment she stood motionless. It was, Mr. Potter thought, quite an entrance.

"Where have you been?" Fischer demanded.

"I was just mailing a letter."

"Don't lie to me. You've been seeing him again."

"Dearest!" She ran forward, hands out-stretched appealingly. On her left arm above the elbow she wore a broad gold band that would have been more appropriate for Cleopatra.

She would never make an actress, Mr. Potter decided. Even with her stunning beauty she was somehow colorless. She lacked any trace of personality, of the kind of vitality that passes like an electric charge across the foot-lights, and she didn't look at the man she was supposed to be addressing. She was staring straight out into the darkened theater.

She leaned forward. "Graham," she called sharply, "make her go away. I won't finish the scene unless she goes away."

Both Collinge and Thornton Grant had risen as she spoke.

"What's wrong, Eve?" Collinge asked.

"That woman! Mrs. Frederick. I won't have her here, spying on me."

Collinge wheeled around, peered at the people behind him. When he saw Cass Grant he caught his breath. Then he observed the white-haired woman who sat quietly in the aisle seat. He went back to Mr. Potter, whispered urgently, "For God's sake, ease her out. Nicely, of course. Eve's going to crack up if she stays."

Eve was standing quite still, for once unconscious of herself, watching. Then her face lighted in a dazzling smile. "Janet! Thanks for coming, darling. Cass dear, how sweet of you. Hi, Pete!" The smile faded. She watched tersely while Mr. Potter made his way along the aisle to Mrs. Maitland Frederick.

Before he could speak to her she got to her feet. She was slightly flushed but her poise was unshaken. Mr. Potter strolled beside her to the door, followed her out into the lobby.

"Is your car waiting?"

She shook her head.

"Then I'll get you a taxi."

"No, I think I'll walk." She smiled faintly. "You are Hiram Potter, aren't you?" The smile faded. "Eve must fear retribution if she sent for you, but I do wish Cass and Janet had stayed away."

"That's good advice."

"But why didn't I follow it myself?" Mrs. Frederick pulled the collar of her fur coat higher around her throat. "I hardly know. I was curious, perhaps, to see how the evil flourish."

She nodded and turned away in dismissal. Mr. Potter waited for her to walk out into the snowstorm but she seemed to be in no hurry. Aware that he was becoming chilled without his overcoat, he went back into the theater.

The first act followed its predictable course. Collinge had done a bold piece of casting by using Howard Mallow, whose virile and so-phisticated charm had been packing women into the theater for years, as the debauched, middle-aged painter. His choice had been more than justified. Mallow and Millicent Cawling, as his wife, made every moment they were on the stage catch fire, in spite of the hackneyed situation. Eve drifted around, with a minimum of lines, looking so beautiful that Mr. Potter was surprised to realize how easily one forgot her when the professionals spoke.

The curtain dropped on act one and Collinge called, "Okay, just a few points and we can go on. Fischer, when you cross right on your last line you're in front of Eve. Wait until you pass the end of the sofa before you start that line. Then it will take you clear to your exit. Eve, darling, look at Fischer when you speak to him, not at the audience. Twice he had to turn his back in order to face you. Come downstage the way we rehearsed it."

"Well, I thought, after all," Eve said in her childish voice, "that since people are coming to look at me —"

"You do it the way you're told, baby, or there won't be any paying customers to look at you after the opening night. That's all. Change for the second act, children."

He stepped on his cigarette, immediately lighted another, and came down the aisle to Mr. Potter.

He grinned. "Uh-huh, don't tell me."

"It's lovely Sardou," Mr. Potter assured him, and ducked.

Collinge sat down beside him. "See the Grants?" he muttered. "What the hell brought them here? And Thornton Grant, too. Damned funny. I hope to God they aren't up to anything. You never can tell with Eve, though. Thrown into a tizzy by Mrs. Frederick and she seemed all bucked up because the Grants were here."

"So I noticed."

"Did you have any trouble with Mrs. Frederick?"

"None at all."

There was a look of alarm on Collinge's face. "Look here, Potter, you don't think she got wind of the plot of this thing, do you? If she's going to be nasty about it —" He broke off as Eve, wearing a sheer dressing gown of green silk, ran out onto the stage.

"Graham!"

At the sound of that shrill voice he muttered, "Now what the hell!" He stood up. "What is it, darling?"

"My black dress for the second act. Someone cut one sleeve all to pieces. It's ruined.

I don't know what —" Her eyes widened. She leaned out over the darkened footlights. "Janet, be a perfect angel and help me, will you? You know about clothes. You have such clever ideas."

"I'll be damned if she will," Cass Grant said explosively.

"For God's sake, hold onto your temper," Pete said in an alarmed voice.

Janet got up quickly, her hand on her brother's arm to quiet him. "I'll help if I can. It's all right, Cass. Don't get upset about it."

"You're a lamb," Eve exclaimed in relief. "You're going to save my life."

"That," Cass said, without troubling to lower his voice, "would be a pity."

Collinge was called away to consult with the photographers who were to take pictures of the cast. The stagehands had taken over again, lowered another backdrop. Thornton Grant went out to the lobby, reaching for his cigarette case. Thornton was not a man to break the law.

Mr. Potter looked around for Cass Grant and his lawyer but they, too, had apparently gone out to stretch their legs.

Sanders Newton stood up, caught sight of Mr. Potter, and came back, beaming.

"Well, Potter, did you buy a piece of this?"

101

"Unfortunately, no. It looks like a smash hit to me."

Newton's broad red face was split by a grin. He rubbed plump hands. "Do I know how to pick 'em! I've never seen Mallow better. Wonderful make-up, isn't it? Now there's a guy I did an injustice. With his handsome pan I never thought he'd agree to do a heavy part, especially one that wrecked his looks. But he jumped at it; said he was tired of being typed and he wanted to act for a change."

"He's the nearest thing to Jean Gabin I've seen on the American stage," Mr. Potter said, "and I know no higher praise."

"Yup. And Eve." The thick lips puckered in an appreciative whistle. "For a hard little piece she manages to look like that fluffy pink sugar candy they sell at Coney Island." He stirred restlessly, a man who always had to be on the move. "Be seeing you. Keep your fingers crossed for the reviews. Maybe the critics will be so stunned by her looks they won't notice that she's a lousy actress." He trotted down the aisle.

Time dragged on. Ten minutes. Twenty.

Thornton Grant was the first to return. He saw Mr. Potter and stopped to speak. "Extraordinary thing, Mrs. Frederick coming here. In all the years our families have known each other she has never been guilty of bad taste."

It occurred to Mr. Potter that Thornton, who accepted Eve's presence in a play that dealt with a murder in which she had been involved, had swallowed an elephant and balked at a gnat.

"I hope you had no unpleasantness with her," Thornton said.

"None at all."

"Did she offer any explanation?"

"For her presence here, you mean? No, but she laid mine to Mrs. Grant's fear of retribution."

"Outrageous!"

Thornton hovered and Mr. Potter watched with some amusement the play of emotion in his face. The face, he suspected, of a man so withdrawn from life that he was not quite real even to himself. But there was genuine conflict in the man now, something moving behind his eyes, twitching the thin lips below the neat mustache. An almost ungovernable curiosity. Thornton yielded to it.

"But why are you here?"

"For the time being, I am Collinge's house guest. He thought it might amuse me."

Thornton did not believe him for a moment. There was open suspicion in his face. Though why Grant should be so curious about his presence; why, indeed, he was here himself was more than Mr. Potter could fathom.

Someone came down the aisle behind them and Thornton scowled. He said, with a minimum of enthusiasm, "Potter, do you know my cousin, Cass Grant?"

Cass did not offer to shake hands. He gave Mr. Potter a swift, unfriendly look and nodded curtly.

There were running feet and Janet raced from the back of the theater, clutched at her brother's arm. He turned as swiftly as a startled deer and Mr. Potter was aware that the man was keyed up, vibrating like an electric wire.

"What's wrong, Jan?"

She was shaking, partly with cold, partly with fright. "The limping man! He was here."

Cass stared at her. "You're sure?"

Her breath was coming in rasping gasps. She nodded. "I found a white lace jacket Eve could wear over the dress to cover —"

"The hell with Eve!"

"Then — it was hot in her dressing room and so many flowers — the heavy perfume made me sick. I went out on the fire escape to get a breath of fresh air, and I heard him walking down in the alley. He was in a hurry, going away. I called him and he ran. I tore down the fire escape and went after him. I caught hold of his coat but he got away."

Cass turned to Thornton. There was an

oddly challenging note in his voice. "She heard the limping man again."

"She says," Thornton remarked nastily. "Janet, this is Mr. Potter. My cousin, Miss Grant. Do tell Potter about your experience, Janet. He is quite an expert at these things."

Janet, trying to steady her breathing, looked at Mr. Potter. Her eyes were even darker than he had realized, and wide either with fright or with intense excitement.

"I've heard about you." Unexpectedly, she held out her hand. "If it's not imposing, I'd like to tell you about it. I think you'd believe me."

"I'll believe you, Miss Grant," he said quietly.

Pete Russlin came down the aisle, triumphantly carrying a bottle of Scotch and three paper cups. "Look children, what papa got for you. Bar around the corner. If we have to sit through this grim clambake, at least we can have our own built-in consolation." He broke off, looking from face to face. "What's happened?"

Collinge had left the stage. The curtains closed. In a moment the footlights went up.

"Curtain!" he called.

And somewhere a woman screamed. Screamed again.

Collinge was the first to race along the side

105

aisle, up the shallow flight of steps that led to the stage. From long familiarity he wove his way around the props, past stagehands in overalls and undershirts, who stood staring; past Fischer who, as usual, got in the way; past Mallow, who was banging on the door of the star's dressing room, shouting, "Open up, for God's sake!"

Collinge pushed the actor aside, flung the door open and then stepped back abruptly, nearly knocking down Thornton Grant who was at his heels.

"God," he choked. "O God!"

Then Mr. Potter was beside him. The dressing room was suffocatingly hot and the air was heavy with the scent of flowers. A gaunt woman with iron-gray hair and a maid's uniform crouched beside Eve, screams tearing from her throat.

Eve crumpled on the floor. Eve with staring eyes and protruding tongue. Eve with a thin noose tight around her throat. Eve with a white card on her breast bearing words whose letters had been cut from newsprint:

"My fatal lady, how do you like this wreath?"

EIGHT

Mr. Potter got up from beside Eve's body. The dresser struggled when he tried to raise her to her feet.

"No," she protested, "I can't leave her."

"There is nothing you can do for her now," he said gently. "She is dead." He helped her up and spoke sharply to Thornton. "Don't touch anything, Grant. Collinge, call the police. You'll all have to get out. Is there a key to this room?"

Slowly they backed out of the room and Mr. Potter locked the door with the key the dresser handed him. He still held the rigid arm, supporting her. After a look at him, Collinge had gone out to the box office to telephone. The rest stood huddled together.

"Where can we wait for the police?" There was an unstressed authority about Mr. Potter that no one ventured to question. Temporarily, at least, he was in charge.

"On the stage, I suppose." Mallow's trained voice easily dominated the confusion. He led the way.

Mr. Potter eased the dresser down on the red plush sofa that had so amused him earlier in the evening. He looked out into the theater

107

where Sanders Newton was standing up, craning in alarm to watch the procession onto the stage, and where the Grants still sat with Pete Russlin.

"What about that Scotch?" Mr. Potter called.

"What's wrong?"

"Eve Grant has been murdered and her dresser is in a state of collapse."

"Good God!" Pete picked up the bottle and started for the stage.

"Will the rest of you join us up here, please?" Mr. Potter's tone was courteous but it did not contemplate a refusal. "No one is to leave the theater until the police give them permission to do so."

Pete was the first on the stage. He poured Scotch into a paper cup and handed it to Mr. Potter, who steadied it as he held it for the dresser, watching in concern the gray color of her skin.

"We could all use some of that," Sanders Newton said. "This is a hell of a thing."

"No more cups," Pete told him.

"There are some in a container backstage. I'll get them," Mallow suggested.

Mr. Potter signaled one of the stagehands. "Perhaps you can find them."

Mallow shot him a quick glance, started to speak, changed his mind. The heavy make-up, the lines of dissipation probably accounted for his malignant expression.

The Scotch circulated in silence, except for Newton's reiterated "This is the hell of a thing."

"My first good part," Fischer burst out petulantly. "This would happen to me!" The look of searing contempt that Millicent Cawling shot at the juvenile lead cut through his almost impervious ego and he stammered in embarrassment. "I'm sure I didn't mean that I'm not sorry about Eve, Sweetie," he said defensively. "Actually, I'm simply shattered. I merely —"

Graham Collinge came back. "Police on their way." He perched on the edge of a table and accepted thankfully the drink Pete Russlin handed him. He looked around from face to face, except, Mr. Potter observed alertly, that he avoided Cass Grant.

So that was it. Inevitable, perhaps. History, apparently, was going to repeat itself. And one person, at least, knew it. Cass Grant, standing behind the cane chair a stagehand had brought for his sister, was leaning on its back as though he needed the support. In his face was sick despair.

Two men came up the aisle toward the lighted stage. Collinge slid off the table.

"Police?" he called into the darkened theater. "I am the one who called you. Graham Collinge."

The two uniformed men from the radio car looked curiously at the motley group on the stage. "Where's the body?"

Mr. Potter handed the playwright the key to Eve's dressing room. The dresser stiffened and then was quiet. No one spoke until Collinge returned, followed by one of the policemen.

"The homicide boys are on their way," the latter said. "Please remain where you are until they give you permission to leave." He leaned against a side wall, standing relaxed and at ease, his eyes roving from face to face, alert when they saw Cass Grant.

"Graham," Millicent said abruptly, "what happened to her?"

It was Thornton Grant who answered. "She was strangled, as Maitland Frederick was strangled." He turned to Janet who had reached up blindly, groping for Cass's hand. "So that's why you claimed to see the limping man tonight, Janet."

The girl looked at him in bewilderment that turned to horror. "Thornton!"

"You hated her," he said venomously. "I always knew that. And you'd shield Cass no matter what he did. You've done that before, haven't you? But you aren't going to get away

110

with that fairy tale a second time."

"By God —" Cass began.

"Quiet!" Mr. Potter's voice was like a whip-lash. "That's a warning. This is no time for accusations."

Pete Russlin had turned to look at Janet and there was naked fear in his face. She met his eyes, her own widening; then she turned to Mr. Potter, as though she were asking a question.

"Mr. Potter, I did hear the limping man tonight. He was in the alley. He must have killed her. And he got away again."

"We'll find him," he said.

"Let's not create any more trouble," Collinge implored them. He drained the drinking cup, crushed it in his fingers, and flung it on the stage. "There's enough hell brewing without stirring up any more."

"But I must insist —" Thornton said.

"Look here, Grant. I can't see that this concerns you," Collinge protested.

"God Almighty! Eve was going to marry me in three weeks." Thornton's voice broke. He dropped onto a chair and buried his face in his hands.

Men tramped down the aisle. "Homicide," the policeman from the radio car said in relief. A doctor with his bag, men with cameras, fingerprint men, quiet efficient specialists in

111

crime detection came up on the stage, headed by the handsomest man on the New York Police Force, Lieutenant O'Toole of Homicide. He looked swiftly around the stage, saw Mr. Potter. Their eyes met and held.

"Let's go," O'Toole said, and Mr. Potter led the way.

The doctor's examination required only a few minutes. "Slipped the noose over her head from the back. She probably didn't even know who it was. The whole thing could have been done in seconds. I don't see anything else. After we get her — oh, there's a fresh bruise here on her upper arm, where the killer must have grabbed her."

Mr. Potter leaned forward, careful not to look at the congested face, but aware of the ugly bruise on her left arm above the elbow. She wore a black dress, from which the left sleeve had been ripped. On the floor beside her lay a white lace jacket.

"That must be why she was wearing that wide gold bracelet on her arm in the first act. To cover that bruise. I wondered at the time why she did that. But in that case, someone manhandled her before the rehearsal started. Her dresser would know. Miss Cawling said someone was in the dressing room here with her; she heard them talking and they wouldn't admit her."

While the fingerprint men and photographers worked and a young sergeant sketched the scene, O'Toole listened and Mr. Potter talked fast.

"Thank God," he concluded, "you're on the case."

"It's going to be a stinker," O'Toole said gloomily. "A real stinker. Cass Grant, ex-husband and ex-murderer; Thornton Grant, husband-to-be; Mrs. Maitland Frederick, with whose husband she had had an affair that led to his killing; Janet Grant, who hated her guts."

"You can eliminate Mrs. Frederick. She left the theater over an hour before the murder was discovered, and apparently Eve had been killed only a matter of minutes before she was found."

"You saw the Frederick woman standing in the lobby," O'Toole pointed out. "You don't know when she left or even if she left."

"It ought to be easy to find someone who saw a white-haired woman wearing evening dress and on foot in this storm."

"Well, at least we know this is going to be Murder One. Whoever left that sign prepared it in advance." O'Toole picked up the white card on which newsprint had been pasted and read it aloud: " 'My fatal lady, how do you like this wreath?' " He turned to the fingerprint man. "Did you find anything on this?"

"No, it was clean."

O'Toole passed it on to one of the men. "See what the lab boys can make of it. Maybe they can get a line on the card. But I can tell you right now where the quotation came from. That's in Horace Gregory's translation of *The Metamorphoses* of Ovid."

Mr. Potter grinned. O'Toole, who looked the way most movie actors would like to look, devoted all his spare time to self-improvement, doggedly working his way through the world's great literature. Then the grin faded.

O'Toole had been watching him. The lieutenant owed his advancement from patrolman to detective and later to his present position to his association with the blond young man who, since that first disastrous murder in which he had been involved, had gradually changed from a negative, retiring man to one whose assurance and authority were obvious at first glance.

"What is it?"

"I was thinking," Mr. Potter said, "that *The Metamorphoses* wouldn't be everyone's dish. That limits the field."

"Whose dish?" O'Toole asked succinctly.

Mr. Potter answered with reluctance, "Thornton Grant is rather well known as

114

a classical scholar."

"Sort of pointing the finger at himself. Still, people do fool things, even the smart ones. Before I talk to them, have you anything else up your sleeve about these people? How did you get in on the ground floor of this one?"

Mr. Potter explained about the malicious mischief to which the dead woman had been subjected. Collinge had thought someone was trying to break her nerve. And that very evening someone had got into her dressing room, cut a sleeve off her second-act costume. Miss Grant had gone, at Eve's request, to help her with her dress.

"Somehow, I don't see her doing anything for Eve Grant. If you remember the trial —"

Mr. Potter remembered it, but he had heard Eve ask Janet to help. She had gone to prevent a scene. O'Toole wanted to know what kind of scene. Cass hadn't liked it, he hadn't wanted his sister to have anything to do with his ex-wife.

"Go on," O'Toole prodded him as Mr. Potter stopped.

Mr. Potter gave a faint shrug. Someone would report that ominous bit of dialogue. It would be better if he did it himself, sound less damning. He did not ask himself why he had developed a strong sense of partisanship for Cass Grant.

"Eve said Janet would save her life and Cass said that would be a pity. A man with murder on his mind wouldn't be such a fool."

"Just crazy, perhaps? Crazy like a fox."

"Miss Grant came back greatly upset. She said she had heard the limping man down in the alley."

"The limping man again!" O'Toole was impatient. "Did you ever see a lame window cleaner? That's what the Grant girl said he was. I didn't believe her at the trial of the Frederick murder case; I don't believe her now. Covering for her brother before the murder was ever discovered. If that isn't collusion, I don't know it when I see it."

"Hey," Mr. Potter said, an unaccustomed sharpness in his tone, "don't go off the deep end on this one, O'Toole. Cass Grant can't have been responsible for the persecution his ex-wife has been suffering for the past weeks, or that bruise on her arm. His party didn't reach the theater until just before the first act started, and she had it by then. Before you lead with your chin, you might consider that there is someone else involved, someone who has been gunning for Eve. Collinge can tell you."

O'Toole surprised him. "There's someone else, all right. That's why I brought Haskel along. Ran into him right after the call came in. He'd had a complaint and he came around to the theater yesterday. Looked the place over. Unless one of the cast was making the trouble, there was only one way an outsider could get at Mrs. Grant's dressing room unseen. Up the fire escape in the alley. He could keep out of sight in a big storeroom next to the window on the fire escape where he could see Eve's door. Haskel set up a plant in the storeroom."

"What did he use? Rhodomin B?"

"Fluoroscin."

"Who made the complaint? Collinge?"

"No, the girl herself. Haskel was bowled over by her." O'Toole broke off to say, "Yes, take her away." He led Mr. Potter out of the room to make space for the men with the basket. "She must have been something to look at before —"

"She was."

"Where is Haskel?"

"Here, sir." The detective carefully kept his eyes off the thing the two men were carrying through the doorway. His face was grim. "If I ever get my hands on the bastard who did that to her I'll vivisect him." He cleared his throat. "I've been checking up in the storeroom. Someone had been in there, moved things a bit but, of course, it could have been stagehands, anyone, for that matter. The window on the fire escape was wide open but that could have been done to indicate an outsider, of course."

"Did you bring that portable apparatus?"

"Yes, sir."

"Wait!" O'Toole called. The men with the basket halted. "Haskel, go over the girl before they take her away."

Haskel's color faded. He swallowed. "Yes, sir."

When Mr. Potter and O'Toole returned to the stage they found the company sitting around quietly, while the policeman leaned against the wall, watching them with open curiosity. The dresser was bolt upright on the sofa, stony-faced, her hands gripping each other, her red-rimmed eyes empty.

Millicent Cawling was busy using cold cream, which a stagehand had brought her, since none of the cast were permitted to leave the stage. She was removing makeup with an unsteady hand. Mallow had already finished and he was patting his face with a wet towel. With the lines of debauchery removed, he emerged as a floridly good-looking man of forty, with full sensual lips and intelligent eyes. Fischer, the juvenile lead, had struck a pose of heartbreak, accentuated by the make-up he had not removed.

Pete Russlin was pouring more drinks for

Collinge and Newton, both of whom were chain-smoking. Thornton Grant sat as though he had not moved, his face still buried in his hands. Janet remained on the cane chair and Cass still stood behind her, so white that Mr. Potter was alarmed.

He spoke in a low voice to O'Toole. "Before the doctor clears out, he'd better take a look at some of these people. It won't help to have them fainting."

O'Toole nodded and passed on word to the policeman.

There was a little stir when Mr. Potter and O'Toole appeared. It was the first time the cast had really seen O'Toole. Millicent Cawling hastily wiped the last of the cream from her face and applied street make-up.

"Ladies and gentlemen, I am Lieutenant O'Toole, in charge of this investigation. I am going to have to ask all of you some questions and I am sure you will give me your full co-operation. Is there any place where we can talk privately?"

"My dressing room," Millicent said. "You can use that."

"Thank you."

"And please have someone bring me my street clothes."

O'Toole spoke to one of the policemen and then looked around him. "First, is there anything any of you can tell me about Mrs. Grant's murder? Anything you saw? Anything you heard?"

Thornton raised his head. "There's no point in wasting your time or our own, Lieutenant. Cass Grant strangled Maitland Frederick. He strangled Eve. There is absolutely no one else."

"Who are you?" O'Toole asked.

"Thornton Grant. And if you want a motive, last night I made the fatal mistake of telling my cousin that Eve was going to marry me."

O'Toole looked at the other man's ravaged face. "You have my deepest sympathy. It is a tragic thing. Have you any evidence to substantiate this charge of yours?"

"Evidence! Good God, man, he killed once, didn't he?"

"If that's all," O'Toole said, "we'll go into it later. Anything else?"

"Someone has been trying —" Collinge began.

O'Toole stopped him with a gesture. "We'll talk to you in a minute, Mr. Collinge." He looked around him. "All right. I must ask you to remain here and not to talk among yourselves. I'll try to let you go home as quickly as possible. It will speed things up considerably if you are willing to co-operate." He nodded to the policeman on guard who pulled up a chair and sat down, folding his arms. "Oh, by the way, do any of you know what family Mrs. Grant had?"

"She was alone in the world," Thornton said.

"I think," Mr. Potter said gently, his hand on the dresser's thin shoulder, "this was her mother."

NINE

"It won't matter to her now," the dresser said dully.

"But I didn't like to hurt Allie — Eve's chances. The Grants are real important socially and she didn't think they would like it. And then — with another fine marriage coming on, she didn't want me around. As family, I mean. How did you guess?"

"Something in the bone structure of your face. A resemblance."

She preceded O'Toole, Mr. Potter and a sergeant with a notebook into Millicent Cawling's dressing room. Unlike the spacious dressing room of the star, this one was narrow, with clothes hanging from a rod along one side, a cluttered make-up table with a brightly lighted mirror, a slipper chair and a shabby armchair.

It pinched Mr. Potter's heart to see the woman automatically clear clothes from the two chairs and hang them carefully before she sat down on the bench at the make-up table. Her hands lay palm upward on her lap. The face she turned to O'Toole was so blank as to appear stupid. She was emptied of emotion.

"What is your name?"

"Simmons. Mrs. Verne Simmons. Eve — my daughter's legal name was Allie Voss. She was my child by my first husband."

Unexpectedly life came back to her face, she beat her clenched fists on her knees. "I shouldn't of left her. Not for a moment. But Miss Grant said to put some snaps on that lace jacket to hold it in place and I went out to the pressing room. Miss Cawling had been using it and everything was out of order, just every which way. It must of taken me a good ten minutes, rummaging around, to find them."

"And when you came back you found your daughter — like that," O'Toole said.

She nodded. Her chin and throat twitched with a kind of spasm at the memory.

The detective was aware that, for the moment, she was incapable of further speech. He waited.

She began to talk abruptly. "Someone was trying to scare her. Things kept happening. I've," her voice broke, "tried my best to protect her."

"Do you know who it was? Or why?"

"No." After a long pause she repeated more firmly, "No."

"Miss Cawling heard someone in your daughter's dressing room before the first act,"

Mr. Potter told her.

"No."

"She heard voices."

"I guess Eve was talking to me."

"How did she get that bruise on her arm?"

"The — murderer —"

Mr. Potter shook his head. "She must have worn that heavy gold band to conceal it. I think the bruise was made before she went on the stage for the first act."

"I — don't know." Mrs. Simmons' voice trailed off.

"Mrs. Simmons," O'Toole said deliberately, "someone choked your daughter to death less than half an hour ago. For God's sake, are you trying to protect her murderer?"

"No," she said hoarsely, "but I can't help her now and I can still protect myself."

"What made you afraid to leave her?" O'Toole asked.

She was thinking hard now. Neither man hurried her, watching her cope with a perplexing problem.

"Someone has been bothering her," she said at last. She was obviously choosing her words carefully, testing them. "Someone kept getting into her dressing room, killing her flowers, putting a dead mouse in the cold cream, a sliver of glass in her powder. It could of disfigured her. Disfigured my beautiful Allie."

A sudden remembrance of the dead girl's congested face as she had last seen it made her fling her hands over her eyes. She began to cry.

The door opened and O'Toole turned around in annoyance that changed to relief. The doctor looked at Mrs. Simmons, put his finger on her pulse and then pushed back the sleeve on a gaunt arm, dabbed it with alcohol, and pressed home the plunger of a hypodermic needle.

"Get her home right away if you can and don't question her tonight," the doctor said firmly.

"But I —" Apathy settled over her again.

O'Toole ordered one of the policemen to take Mrs. Simmons home. She was to rest tonight. He'd see her tomorrow.

When the woman had gone, O'Toole said, "She knows a lot she isn't telling. Ten to one she could finger the killer, if she weren't scared half out of her wits. I'll have to get it out of her tomorrow when she is more fit to talk. Make her see it's the only way she can be safe."

"What about tonight?" Mr. Potter asked quietly.

O'Toole called to a policeman outside the door, ordered a guard for Mrs. Simmons for the night and then said, "Get Collinge in

125

here next, will you?"

The playwright came promptly and, after a quick, uneasy look around him, relaxed. He sat down, stretched out his legs and gave a long sigh. Then he looked at Mr. Potter.

"Just how responsible am I for this?" he demanded. "If I hadn't got the idea of a melodrama based on the Frederick murder, with Eve acting in it, would all this have happened?"

"I don't know," Mr. Potter admitted soberly.

"But there's a connection?"

"Well, it's carrying coincidence rather far to think that two principals in the Frederick case should die in the same way if there is no connection."

Collinge sighed again. "And to think Simmons was Eve's mother! *De mortuis* and all that, but Eve was not a very nice person. She led that woman a dog's life. Simmons waited on her hand and foot." A third sigh. "Well, Lieutenant, what can I tell you?"

Under O'Toole's questioning he described the series of contretemps that had wrought Eve up to the point of hysteria. And it hadn't, he pointed out, been confined to the theater. She'd been getting almost no sleep because of the constant telephone calls at her apartment. Yes, of course, he knew where she lived.

126

He felt in his pocket for a small address book, found the number, an apartment building on Central Park West.

"What do you make of this?" O'Toole asked.

"I think Eve knew who was doing it," Collinge said bluntly. "She was scared silly."

"Like her mother," the detective commented. "Did she tell you she called the police yesterday about it?"

Collinge jerked up his head in surprise. "She did! No, she didn't say a word to me about it. Did they find anything?"

O'Toole explained about the plant that Haskel had set up in the storeroom. Anyone hiding in there would be almost bound to pick up some traces of the stuff.

"So that's why that guy of yours has been going over everyone on the stage!"

"All right," O'Toole said. "Find anything?"

"They're all clean except for the Grant girl. Fluoroscin showed up on her fingertips."

"The girl!" O'Toole said in surprise. "I'd have put my money on the brother. Unless she was staked out, on guard, so he could get in and out of the dressing room unseen." He nodded to Haskel. "Okay. That's all."

He turned back to the playwright. "Now, Mr. Collinge, suppose you tell me about the people in your cast, their relations with the dead woman, and where they were from — oh, say when they started coming to the theater this evening."

They'd have to ask the stage manager, Collinge explained. He and Mr. Potter hadn't reached the theater until a few minutes before the dress rehearsal was scheduled to begin. By then, the actors were all presumably dressing. The stagehands certainly could be eliminated.

No one could be eliminated at this point, O'Toole told him.

The cast — Collinge's lips compressed, puckered, compressed again. "So far as I know, there was no real enmity," he said slowly. "Millicent Cawling had no use for Eve but that was chiefly because the gal simply didn't know the rudiments of acting and she deliberately stole a scene every chance she got, moved a hand or a handkerchief, or something like that. Any professional would find such shenanigans hard to swallow."

"How about the men?"

"Well, not Fischer certainly." Collinge grinned. "Mallow? He might have made a few passes. He probably did. With almost any good-looking woman he invariably did. And, hell, you've seen Eve!"

"Not alive," O'Toole reminded him rather grimly.

Collinge sobered. "No. Of course not. But Eve — she was spectacularly beautiful. As close to perfect beauty as I've ever seen. God, what a criminal waste!" He observed the speculative look on the detective's face. He was startled and then, unexpectedly, he laughed outright.

"Oh, no! I wasn't interested in Eve. I have my own interests. Besides, can you conceive of any playwright doing in his leading lady the night before what looks like a smash hit? Be your age, man. Anyhow," he added cheerfully, "Wilson, the stage manager, can account for my movements from the time I got here."

He looked at his watch. "If you don't need me any more right now, I'd like to put in some good work on Sanders Newton. Try to sweeten him up. He bought damned near fifty per cent of this piece and he must be pawing the ground."

O'Toole nodded. "That will be all for tonight. I'll want to see you again tomorrow, of course."

"Have a heart, man. Don't make it before noon."

"Send in Thornton Grant, will you?"

Mr. Potter intervened quickly. "Why don't you see Miss Grant first? Thornton is hell-bent on sending one or both of his cousins to the chair for this."

"I'm not sure I blame him." O'Toole looked

129

at Mr. Potter. "Okay, make it Miss Grant then. And, Collinge, don't say anything about the fluoroscin, will you?"

Collinge nodded and went out. In a moment a policeman stuck his head around the door. "That fellow Russlin is raising a stink. He says he won't permit Miss Grant to talk to you except in the presence of her lawyer. You want to see her alone?"

"I want to see her alone," O'Toole answered.

In a couple of minutes Janet appeared in the doorway. She was very pale. Her eyes looked enormous and much too bright. The two men stood up.

"Sit down, Miss Grant," O'Toole said.

She sat down, her feet braced, hands gripping the arms of her chair, as though prepared for a dentist's drill.

"Suppose," O'Toole said quietly, "you tell us in your own words what happened tonight. Everything."

Janet frowned, trying to marshal her thoughts. When she spoke she addressed Mr. Potter. "It really started last night. Yesterday, my brother Cass was released from Wentworth. His lawyer, Pete Russlin, and I drove him down to our house on Sixty-eighth Street."

She described the arrival, after dinner, of

Thornton, who had tried to persuade Cass to leave the country and change his name.

"And Cass said," Janet's chin went up proudly, "that he didn't intend to change his name, he intended to clear it."

Then Eve had come, and she had said she was going to marry Thornton. Thornton, of all people!

"What was your brother's reaction to that, Miss Grant?"

"He simply roared with laughter. Thornton was fuming, especially after Cass said that, after all, Thornton has all his money now as well as his own; nothing surprising in Eve's wanting to get her hands on it if she could."

"And your sister-in-law?" O'Toole asked.

Janet still continued to address Mr. Potter as though they were alone in the room. "There was something queer about that. Thornton certainly was surprised when Eve came. And after what she had done to Cass, we were rocked off our feet to think she dared put in an appearance in our house."

"But if she was engaged to marry your cousin, why did she come to see her ex-husband?"

"That's just what Cass said after they left, Eve and Thornton. He wondered what she was really after. It was the queerest thing. I

131

think she was scared half to death when she got there."

"What did she want?" O'Toole said. "A reconciliation?"

"Good heavens, no! Cass hated the very sight of her." She broke off, aghast. "But he wasn't jealous of Thornton. Of his own free will, he'd never have set eyes on Eve again."

"And yet he came here tonight," O'Toole pointed out.

Janet leaned forward, speaking eagerly. "But, don't you see, that's what was so queer. Eve begged us to come. Literally. She went down on her knees beside my chair. You can ask Thornton. Even he would have to admit that."

"Why did she do that?"

"I don't know," Janet admitted helplessly. "She said if we came tonight it would help to prevent any more gossip when she married Thornton. It would show we were all friends, no hard feelings. Cass absolutely refused. It was Pete, Cass's lawyer and his best friend, Pete Russlin, who persuaded us. He said it might be the best thing to do, in the long run. But —"

Mr. Potter spoke quietly. "What puzzles you so much, Miss Grant?"

"The strangest thing about it was that I was the one Eve really wanted here tonight. Not

Cass. She was trying to tell me something. She said I'd be glad I came. She promised I'd be glad. There was something —" Her hands made a helpless gesture, dropped to the arms of her chair.

"Now about tonight," O'Toole said briskly.

"Cass and Pete and I had dinner and then we came here to the theater. It was just before the rehearsal began. And then —" She described Eve's hysterical attack on Mrs. Frederick. "After that, they went through the first act. We were just sitting there when Eve came running out on the stage. Her second-act costume had been spoiled. You know about that?"

O'Toole nodded.

"And," Janet said triumphantly, "Cass couldn't have done that. We were together from the time we sat down to dinner until Eve came running out on the stage. Pete had dinner with us. He can tell you. Well, Eve asked if I would help her. I didn't want to but I thought maybe she'd have a chance to explain why she had insisted on my coming here. I've always believed she knew who really killed Mr. Frederick. And she certainly knew the limping man."

"Go on," O'Toole said, appearing not to hear the challenge in her voice.

"Well, I went to her dressing room and I

saw that a sleeve had been cut off the dress. Just slashed. Her dresser — oh, it's her mother, poor thing! — was terribly upset. I tried to question Eve but she wouldn't say anything except about the dress."

She broke off, frowning. "I don't know why I didn't think of that before. The black dress she had on, with the sleeve cut up — it wasn't a new dress."

"What about it?" O'Toole asked with a look of impatience.

"But, don't you see, this was her first starring part, and anyhow Eve adored clothes. She'd never have planned to wear an old one." She looked up at the two waiting men. "Do you suppose," she asked slowly, "she did it herself? Cut up that dress as an excuse to get me backstage?"

"And why would she do that?" O'Toole was noncommittal. "At least it is an original theory."

She shook her head. "It doesn't make sense because when I got there she didn't say anything, didn't explain."

"As you say, it doesn't make sense," O'Toole said.

She became aware belatedly of his patent disbelief. Her shoulders stiffened. "Just the same, I'll bet there is another black dress somewhere."

"Why don't you have a look?" O'Toole suggested.

She went carefully along the line of dresses, the white evening dress for the first act, a red velvet housecoat, a plain tailored blue linen suit that looked as though it had been designed for a sixteen-year-old schoolgirl, the street clothes which Eve had worn to the theater.

"Shall we go on?" O'Toole asked politely.

Janet came back to her chair. She was flushed now and angry. She waited a moment to be sure that her voice would be under control.

"I found a lace jacket to cover the damage. We tried it on. It needed some snaps and Mrs. Simmons said she would get them. So — that's all. There was nothing more for me to do. It was hot in there and the perfume from those masses of flowers was so heavy it made me sick. And I didn't like Eve, anyhow."

"Just a minute," Mr. Potter interrupted for the first time. "Did you notice anything when you were helping Eve with that black dress?"

The big dark eyes asked a question. "I don't know what you mean. What sort of thing?"

"When did she take off that wide gold band she wore above her left elbow?"

"Oh, of course. I'd thought during the first act that it was just another evidence of her bad taste. But when Mrs. Simmons unfastened the bracelet for her there was an ugly bruise on her arm. She had been trying to cover it up."

Janet thought, her brow furrowed. Mrs. Simmons had told Eve that she would get some Covermark cream next morning, the kind of thing people use to conceal birthmarks, so the bruise wouldn't show on the opening night.

"Then Mrs. Simmons lied to us about the bruise," Mr. Potter commented to O'Toole.

The latter grunted. "She lied about a number of things but she was in no state to put pressure on her." He turned back to Janet. "Was Mrs. Grant alone when you left her?"

"Yes, Mrs. Simmons had gone to find the snaps. And Eve was alive, Lieutenant. I swear to you that she was alive."

"Then what did you do?"

"I went out on the fire escape for a breath of fresh air."

"Was the window hard to open?" O'Toole asked casually.

"Oh, no, it was wide open. Then, down in the alley, I heard the halting steps of the limping man. I tore down that fire escape and ran. I called to him. I even touched the back of his coat, but he pulled away and by the time I reached the street —" She made a despairing gesture. "There were a number of people scurrying along with their heads down

136

in the snow. I didn't know which one he was."

"Are you trying to make me believe he killed your sister-in-law?"

There was anger in Janet's face. "I'm not trying to make you believe anything. Just reporting exactly what happened. Anyhow, I realize now that he couldn't have killed her. He was going away from the theater and Eve was still alive."

"I see." O'Toole's tone was noncommital. "Now perhaps you will tell me why you were in the storeroom. Is that where you found the lace jacket?"

"No, it was in Eve's dressing room."

"Then how," O'Toole demanded, cold eyes on her face, "did you get that fluoroscin on your fingertips?"

"The stuff that glowed when the detective used that little portable machine? But I don't know." Janet looked at her fingers as though expecting to find the answer there.

"That's what we call a plant," O'Toole said. "It was set up yesterday in the storeroom to trap the person who has been causing so much trouble for Mrs. Grant. As you see, it's a stain, and it is extremely difficult to remove."

"But I never saw the storeroom," Janet protested, aghast. "I don't even know where it is."

"Perhaps," O'Toole said, "you would find

it easier to remember if we took you down-town for questioning."

Mr. Potter intervened in a low tone. "Don't arrest her now, O'Toole, for God's sake. There's something damned queer going on. Personally, I never believed her brother killed Frederick. Someone is sure as hell gunning for the Grants. After Cass's conviction, this girl won't have the chance of a snowball in hell. Keep it open for twenty-four hours."

"You're taking this as hard," O'Toole said in surprise, "as though you had a personal stake in it."

" 'Every man's death diminishes me,' " Mr. Potter quoted.

O'Toole wasn't satisfied. Damned, he thought in consternation, if the poor guy hasn't fallen in love again — and with another murderess at that.

TEN

When the taxi pulled up before the 68th Street house Janet said impulsively, "Will you come in?"

Mr. Potter hesitated. "Hadn't you better get some rest?"

Rest! After the past months of strain, worrying about Cass's release; the ugliness of his homecoming the night before, the hostile crowds, the stone through the window; and then — unbelievably — Eve; the horror of the past evening climaxed by Eve's murder, she was bone-weary, numb with exhaustion. But — rest?

"Not until Cass comes home. I couldn't possibly."

Mr. Potter's very blue eyes searched her face and then he held out his hand for the key.

"Thank you," she said shakily.

There was a sandwich tray waiting in the library with drinks and a tub of ice.

Janet dropped onto the couch before the cold grate in which a fire had been laid, her coat wrapped tightly around her, although the house was warm.

Mr. Potter, moving quietly in the background, mixed her a drink and brought her a sandwich which she refused. He stuck a match in the fire and set the plate of sandwiches and a tall glass on the small table in front of him. He bit into a sandwich, waiting for her to speak.

"What's going to happen now?" she asked at length.

"Talk," he said. "A great deal of it. Questions and more questions."

"How long?"

"Until the police arrive at the truth."

"The way they did before?" When he made no comment she burst out, "They'll arrest Cass. Start the whole ugly thing over again. Why did I do it? Why did I get him out of Wentworth? At least he was safe there. Nothing more could have happened to him. Oh, God! Why didn't I let him alone?"

"Aren't you borrowing trouble?" asked the quiet man beside her.

"Then why wouldn't they let me wait for him at the theater?"

"They prefer seeing one witness at a time. O'Toole thought you'd be better off at home."

"That's not true, is it? He was going to take me to the police station. He didn't believe a word I said. If it hadn't been for you —" She stretched out her hands, looking at the fingertips that had betrayed her. "That stain, I

140

don't understand it at all. How did I get it?"

"It's what, in crime detection, is called a plant, a chemical substance used to trap a suspect. It adheres to the skin or the clothing. They use something that hasn't a noticeable texture, not oily or greasy or sticky. Something a person cannot feel or see but that, under the light of an ultraviolet tube, will glow brightly. They call it tracing when the suspect touches the article on which the plant has been placed and it sticks to his clothing or his skin. Washing it off is extremely difficult."

To the listening girl his voice sounded flat and pedantic, like a teacher reading a lesson.

"Yesterday," he went on, "Mrs. Grant called the police about a series of mishaps that had occurred in her dressing room at the theater and the plant was set up in the theater's storeroom, the only place where anyone could be concealed and still be able to keep an eye on her dressing room."

"But I never saw the storeroom, Mr. Potter. I swear it."

"What exactly did you touch?"

She thought back. The events of less than three hours ago seemed to have happened in the immeasurable past. "The black dress, of course. Actually, that's about all. Mrs. Simmons moved the costumes on the hangers so

141

I could see what was there. I picked out the lace jacket. Oh, I handled that, too. Nothing else in the room. I left as soon as I could. The window was wide open, so I stepped out on the fire escape; I held the railing when I ran down, but only with my left hand and it's on — Mr. Potter, the back of the limping man's coat! I touched him with both hands!"

"Tell me about the limping man," Mr. Potter suggested. "But, first, eat one of these sandwiches."

"I can't."

"Yes, you can."

To her surprise, Janet found that she could. When she finished it, she reached for another. "Well, I feel better."

He smiled suddenly. "Never try to face problems on an empty stomach. How much dinner did you eat?"

She shrugged slim shoulders. "We were keyed up, you know, and Cass hated the very idea of going. He only went along because he wouldn't allow me to do it alone."

"Then why did you go, Miss Grant?"

"Because there was something about Eve, as though she were trying to give me a message. She said she'd promise me I'd be glad I came. That was true, even if the lieutenant didn't believe me."

"But you believed her."

The comment was noncommittal but it made her say sharply, "Yes, I did. Because she hadn't wanted to come here, to face Cass after wrecking his life. She was scared to death. It would take something terribly important to make her do it. I had the strangest feeling —"

"Well?"

"That she knew who had killed Maitland Frederick and she intended to tell me."

"But why didn't she tell you while she was here at the house?"

"I don't know. Unless it was something she didn't want Thornton to hear. He's terribly virtuous and filled with all those New England qualities that are so hard to bear. So self-righteous. She hadn't expected to find him in this house because he never liked Cass much."

Mr. Potter got up to throw another log on the fire. "Does it seem likely to you, Miss Grant, that your sister-in-law would be planning to marry a man she was afraid of?"

"Good heavens, she wasn't afraid of Thornton! She was afraid to have him find out something." Janet set down her empty glass and took off her coat. She was warmer now.

Mr. Potter turned to her and smiled. "Wouldn't you like to hazard a wild guess as to what that visit was all about?"

"All right. I think Eve left something in this house, something she lost or mislaid, and she's absolutely terrified of having it found. Someone has repeatedly broken in — you can ask Marker, our caretaker, if you like — and Eve was the only one, except for me, who still had keys at the time I closed up the house. She'd been looking for something. I'm sure of it. And she never expected we'd live here again. Now that we've come back —"

"Were you so much in each other's confidence that she would tell you about it?"

Janet's hands dropped helplessly. "You don't believe me either. Of course we were never close. I never trusted her. But if the thing she knew would clear Cass I think she'd have taken a chance on me. Fair exchange, of course," she added bitterly. "Eve wanted something and she'd have given me some information to pay for it."

"Which she failed to do," Mr. Potter reminded her.

Janet pulled herself wearily up from the couch but there was quiet dignity in the drawn white face. "It was kind of you to bring me home," she said in a tone of dismissal.

With gentle hands he thrust her back on the couch. "I have to know," he told her. "If I am going to help you, I have to know. Don't

144

lose faith in me when I probe the painful spots." One of his hands covered hers. "You remember, I told you earlier this evening that I would believe you."

She nodded.

"Look at me," he said, and for a long moment they looked into each other's eyes steadily, probing deep. Her eyes widened with a shock of surprise. Mr. Potter removed his hand as though it burned, removed himself as well, went to pull up a chair facing her, took a moment settling himself.

Janet was the first to recover her poise. There was something new in her voice when she spoke, something like a stirring of hope. "It seems to me the main thing to do is to look for someone who is — well, unhinged, or who has so strong a reason for hating Eve that he could do a thing like that in a moment of hot-blooded impulse."

"But this," Mr. Potter told her, "wasn't a crime of hot-blooded impulse, Miss Grant. It was cold-blooded and premeditated."

"What makes you think that?" she demanded sharply.

"Because there was a card lying on her breast, made up of letters cut from newsprint. That required time and forethought. It read," his eyes came back to her face but the expression that had temporarily transformed them and warmed her heart was gone, they seemed singularly cold: " 'My fatal lady, how do you like this wreath?' "

There was nothing to be read in her face but blank surprise.

"O'Toole," and Mr. Potter smiled, "is a demon for self-improvement, who devotes his leisure time to the classics. He recognized the quotation. It's to be found in Horace Gregory's translation of *The Metamorphoses* of Ovid."

Janet started as though she had touched a live wire, the color draining out of her face.

"You've read it?" he asked.

Her lips parted without sound.

"Put your head down," he said sharply. "Way down! That's right." He was beside her on the couch again, his fingers finding the pulse that leaped and raced erratically in her wrist.

Little by little, it steadied and she raised her head. Mr. Potter slid an arm around her to support her. With a feeling of rest she leaned against his shoulder. Then she turned to look up into his face. It was very near her own. He bent over and kissed her.

What began as a fleeting gesture of comfort, of sympathy, was like a match dropped into a keg of powder. His mouth on hers was insistent, demanding, and she found herself responding with an ardor that surprised her. She raised her arms and locked them around his neck.

When his unexpectedly strong hold relaxed on her body, which had leaped to meet his, he spoke, scarcely lifting his lips from hers. "I didn't mean to do this. For God's sake, what's happened to us?"

"I don't know." Her lips brushed his as she spoke. "I don't care."

His mouth fastened on hers again, until she pushed him away, breathless.

"Let me breathe," she said, laughing and unashamed, her face warm and glowing, black eyes shining.

He released her and stood up. "O'Toole will be in touch with you tomorrow," he said rapidly. "If possible, I'll try to be with him. In any case, you can reach me at Graham Collinge's apartment." He added, as he caught up his hat and overcoat, like a man in flight, "That is, if you need me, of course."

Without another word he went out of the library. In a few moments she heard the outer door close.

For a long time she sat motionless before the dying fire. Little by little, her expression altered, became thoughtful, alert, wary.

"I wonder," she said aloud in the quiet room. She began to shake. "But it couldn't be that. There was nothing I said —"

The sharp sound of the telephone brought her bolt upright. She ran to stop the ringing.

When Collinge's man servant had opened the door and taken Mr. Potter's hat and coat, he went into the big living room, which seemed to be filled with people all talking at once. Actually, only three men were there: Collinge himself, busy at the bar; Pete Russlin, pacing the floor; and Sanders Newton, who was at the telephone arguing passionately with the publicity agent for *Fatal Lady*.

Collinge hailed his guest with an unsuccessful attempt to be jovial. He waved a hand. "Behold three men who — so far — have escaped the chair. I brought Newton and Russlin along to ply them with liquor. Help yourself."

Mr. Potter poured Haig & Haig and settled himself in a deep chair.

"What happened after I left?"

"All hell broke loose," Collinge told him, the fake good cheer dropping away. "Wilson, my stage manager, was able to clear all the stagehands and me, thank God! Fischer's okay and in the clear. That good-looking lieutenant pounded away at Millicent, but all she could say was that someone had been in Eve's dressing room before the first act and Simmons refused to open the door."

Collinge paused to make an effect. "And not one other damn person has an alibi that's worth a hoot. Not a single one! Mallow hadn't finished changing for the second act, though he had had far more time than he'd get at a regular performance. He claimed he was telephoning, but there's only one phone in the place and Newton was using that. He says." He grinned maliciously.

"Damn it," Newton began, and then laughed it off.

"Mrs. Frederick may have left the theater and she may not. O'Toole is checking to see whether any one saw her before he questions her. And, O dear God! I made her the murderer! Russlin here says he was around the corner at a bar getting a bottle of Scotch. Thornton and Cass Grant both claimed they had been smoking in the lobby. But each of them denies the other was there. Thornton raised holy hell. Acted like a madman. He kept yelling at Cass, 'You won't get out of this one!' Turned on Russlin and said, 'How much did the Grants pay you to get Cass off the first time?' It was hell, I tell you. Blazing hell. And O'Toole letting them talk, taking it all in."

"So how did it end?" Mr. Potter asked.

Collinge shrugged. "The police told me politely that I could go home. I collected

Newton. Then Russlin raised a howl when O'Toole started on Cass Grant, so the police kicked him out and I brought him along here."

"How about Thornton?"

"They sent him home, too, but I included him out."

Collinge's soft-footed servant came in to answer the telephone. "Mr. Potter," he said, collected empty glasses, dumped cluttered ashtrays, and went out.

It was O'Toole speaking. "Thought I might find you there. Know where I can reach Russlin? He's not at his apartment."

"He's right here." Mr. Potter was aware of three alert heads turned in his direction, of growing tension.

"Cass Grant wants him."

"At the theater?"

"No, we're holding him for questioning." After fractional pause O'Toole said, "Sorry, Potter." There was something very like pity in his voice.

ELEVEN

That night, in spite of the disaster that had overtaken his leading lady and his play, Graham Collinge slept with the relief of a man who had been cleared of all complicity in the crime. He was still sleeping when Mr. Potter dressed and left the apartment early the next morning.

Mr. Potter had not slept at all. For hours he had paced the floor, deeply shaken by his spontaneous flare-up of passion for Janet Grant. It was years since any woman had had such an effect on him. Then it had ended in tragedy. This time — part of his mind remained detached, coldly analytical. The spark that had set off the conflagration had followed his comment about the Ovid quotation. If she wanted to produce a distraction, he thought grimly, she had succeeded beyond her wildest hopes.

He forced himself to push away the disturbing thought of the responsive girl in his arms and went over the events of the evening. Within a day or two, the painstaking O'Toole would be able to establish the whereabouts of some, at least, of the people implicated: Cass Grant, Thornton Grant, Janet Grant,

151

Mrs. Maitland Frederick, Pete Russlin, Sanders Newton, Howard Mallow. Seven people who could not account satisfactorily for their activities at the time of the murder; who, so far, had provided no real corroboration for their statements. Janet Grant's fingertips had been stained with fluoroscin. She denied ever having been in the storeroom; instead, she claimed to have touched the limping man. Obviously O'Toole regarded the latter as the joker in the deck but she had been genuinely shaken when she ran down the aisle to her brother. Unless — he pushed that thought away, too.

At this point, no one could be eliminated, but at least the likelihood that Sanders Newton had strangled Eve was remote. He had sunk a lot of money in *Fatal Lady*. He had been exuberant over the chances of success, and certainly he had not betrayed any personal interest in Eve beyond a normal man's response to her beauty. Of course, there was always the possibility that he had been involved with her in the past. The chances were that Eve's multiple love life would have staggered a Tibetan woman.

Mallow? According to Collinge, the actor wasn't apt to overlook an opportunity where women were concerned. Mr. Potter shook his head, dissatisfied. In his experience, men who had a long succession of affairs were unlikely to be deeply involved with any particular woman; they were rarely capable of total commitment. Still it would be interesting to know why he had not had time to dress for the second act. How long had the intermission been? Twenty minutes, at least.

Mrs. Frederick? Mr. Potter stopped his restless pacing. She and Mrs. Simmons were the only persons among the group who had not been tested for fluoroscin. Of course, O'Toole would think of that.

Mr. Potter showered, dressed, and let himself quietly out of the apartment. Snow had stopped falling but the sky was a dull gray. In the night, plows had cleared the streets, leaving dirty piles of snow around the cars parked at the curb. The sidewalks had been partially cleared. Only Central Park wore a white crown proudly, so far unsmirched by city filth.

At the first drugstore, Mr. Potter slid on a stool and ordered coffee. When he had finished it he picked up newspapers at a kiosk and hailed a cab. He gave the address and the cabdriver cocked an eyebrow.

With the exception of *The New York Times*, Eve's picture appeared on the front page of all the papers. Eve in evening dress, entering Twenty-One. Eve from a cabinet photograph, looking seraphic and stunningly beautiful. Eve at her husband's trial dressed like a schoolgirl, and looking frozen with fear. Mr. Potter stared at that picture for a long time before he turned to the story.

EVE GRANT MURDERED
EX-HUSBAND HELD FOR
QUESTIONING

Eve Grant, famous beauty and key figure in the Maitland Frederick murder trial of four years ago, was strangled last night in her dressing room at the Crescent Theater during the dress rehearsal of *Fatal Lady*, which was to have opened this evening. (See p. 14 for story about Graham Collinge, the playwright.)

The play was alleged to deal with the Frederick murder case and Eve Grant, according to advance stories, was to play the role she had enacted in life.

The murder was discovered by her dresser, Mrs. Simmons. Cass Grant, millionaire playboy, whom she divorced after he was incarcerated for life as criminally insane, was freed only thirty-six hours before the murder, after a long legal battle with his sister, Janet Grant, and comprehensive examinations by the famous Swiss alienist, Dr. Franz Beldner. (See p. 28 for special article on psychiatrists and some alleged criminals whom they have been responsible for having released from prison.)

Mr. Grant was accompanied to the theater by his lawyer, Peter Russlin, whose sensational defense tactics enabled Grant to escape the chair in the Frederick murder trial.

Thornton Grant, cousin of Cass Grant, a distinguished classical scholar, made a statement to this reporter. He had planned to marry the beautiful actress within three weeks. It was this information, he believed, that had induced Mrs. Grant's former husband, his sister and his lawyer to attend the dress rehearsal which ended so tragically. Miss Janet Grant (picture on p. 3), known five years ago as the most beautiful debutante of a generation, is the last person known to have seen the actress alive.

Mr. Potter turned to page three and studied the face of the girl who smiled back at him. The picture had been taken at her debut. She was young, trusting, and lovely, but unlike the wary young woman whom he had met the night before, unlike the passionate woman whom he had taken in his arms.

He pushed away the newspapers. Thornton Grant was determined to send his cousin, or cousins, to the chair. So much had been apparent the night before. Thornton and his classical scholarship. Thornton and the Ovid quotation. Thornton who had no alibi. And yet the man had been grief-stricken. Only intense emotion could explain his public breakdown.

The cabdriver said irritably, "Look, mister! This is where you wanted to go, isn't it? I keep telling you and —"

Mr. Potter sat up with a start. "Oh, sorry." He glanced at the meter, added a tip. "I wasn't thinking."

The driver saw the paper. "Didja see her pitcher? Gorgeous! I hope they get the bastard this time — and good. Let 'em off once and they kill again. If I had my way, a guy like that would be lynched."

Mr. Potter started to speak, let it go. The cabdriver, at the moment, voiced public opinion. At the moment, Cass Grant had already been convicted. Without a miracle he wouldn't have a chance. Mr. Potter had little faith in miracles. His face was grim when he walked into the building and inquired for Lieutenant O'Toole.

The latter was already at his desk, in spite

156

of the early hour, a cardboard carton of coffee beside him, ashtray overflowing with cigarette butts. He looked as though he hadn't slept at all though, as usual, he was cleanly shaven. He nodded and waved to a battered chair. He sipped coffee, grimaced and set it down. "Cold," he said in disgust.

"When did you get to bed?" Mr. Potter asked.

"I caught a couple of hours on the couch down here." The lieutenant eyed his friend rather cautiously, waiting for an outburst of protests.

"I suggest we go out for breakfast," Mr. Potter said mildly.

O'Toole pushed himself up from his chair, hands on the desk. "That's an idea. I was thinking of calling you. I'd like you to go with me when I see Mrs. Frederick. You know how to handle her kind. Anyhow, you're observant and you would remember what clothes she wore last night. We'll take Haskel along."

While the two men disposed of ham and eggs, to which O'Toole added an order of pancakes, they maintained a companionable silence. When he had drained his third cup of coffee, the lieutenant sat back with a sigh of repletion.

An official car was waiting for them. A police sergeant sat beside the driver; Haskel, with his portable machine, got in back with the other two men. O'Toole gave the Central Park West address of Eve Grant. As the car slid through traffic he began to talk about the night's activities. Eve Grant's background was being raked over with a finetooth comb. The stagehands had been cleared; they hadn't been out of sight or sound of each other during the crucial times. That applied to Collinge, too.

The cast seemed to be okay. Mallow had given them some trouble at first. He had probably had a passing affair with Eve, though he wouldn't admit it, but he had broken down finally and explained why he had not dressed for the second act. He had a crippling arthritis and his dresser had been working on him. He didn't want it known. His career rested heavily on his sexual appeal; a rumor that he was physically unfit would do his reputation irreparable damage. His dresser had backed his story and Mallow had, without hesitation, given them the doctor's name. Someone would get on him this morning.

Sanders Newton had turned over a list of people whom he had called during the interval and that had checked: A guy on *Variety*, one on the *News*, one on the *American*. They all said he had been beating the drum for *Fatal Lady*. The calls would have taken up the

158

whole crucial period.

O'Toole broke off to curse under his breath. Waiting below the canopy of the big apartment building on Central Park West there were a dozen men with cards in their hatbands, ignoring the protests of the uniformed doorman.

"Jackals," O'Toole muttered.

Mr. Potter eyed his handsome friend in some amusement. The most photogenic and one of the hardest-working of New York's Finest got no satisfaction from personal publicity.

As O'Toole stepped out of the car, cameras snapped and a chorus of voices rose. He held up his hand.

"Nothing new to report, boys. We'll issue a statement as soon as we have anything for you."

"What about Cass Grant?"

"He's not under arrest. We're holding him for questioning, that's all."

"How come his sister was with Eve? She's been fighting her for four years."

"No comment."

The police forced their way through the crowd of reporters and cameramen, carrying Mr. Potter along with them, like a piece of birchbark floating on a wave. The lobby was ostentatious rather than handsome but it represented, Mr. Potter thought, Eve's taste. The door of her apartment was opened by a policeman who had been sitting in a chair in the hallway. Big as it was, the living room gave an impression of clutter. There were too many elaborate lamps, too many small cushions, too many ornaments. There were flowers everywhere. Stacked on the floor around a record player were jazz recordings and albums of Broadway musicals. The pictures on the wall were all of Eve herself.

The policeman who had admitted them said the fingerprint men had already gone over the place. No one had come except a reporter who had got in by claiming to be an electrician. Mrs. Grant had a colored maid who came by the day but she wasn't expected to report until ten and she always left by seven.

The bedroom had a canopied bed with a headboard of tufted pink satin. There were ruffled pink curtains at the windows, a white velvet rug on the floor. Clothes were scattered over chairs and chaise longue. A room-length closet on one side revealed, beyond sliding doors, a wardrobe that stopped the men in their tracks. On perfumed hangers, against walls of more tufted pink satin, were suits, street dresses, afternoon dresses, evening dresses, furs — mink and sable and ermine.

"Where in the name of God did she get

the money?" O'Toole demanded. "She hadn't drawn much alimony from Cass Grant. His father had cut him off with three hundred dollars a month for life and turned over his entire fortune to Thornton."

"Wait," the policeman who had been on guard said dryly, "until you get a load of the john."

The bathroom had mirrored walls and a sunken tub of pink marble.

"Well," O'Toole declared as they returned to the bedroom, "she was certainly doing all right in her own way."

A key turned in the outside lock and the door was opened by an attractive colored girl. She seemed neither surprised nor alarmed by their presence. For a moment she looked at the men and then she addressed Mr. Potter.

"I am Mrs. Grant's maid, Helen Baxter," she said quietly.

"This is Lieutenant O'Toole, Miss Baxter. He's the one in charge of the investigation."

"You knew about this?" O'Toole asked.

"It was on television with the eleven o'clock news last night and I saw the morning paper."

"Suppose we sit down in the living room where we can be comfortable," O'Toole suggested. "Now then, Miss Baxter, what can you tell us?"

She sat down composedly, her hands relaxed

on her lap. She had, Mr. Potter thought, highly intelligent eyes.

"There's not much I can tell you. Nothing about the murder, of course. And I have never been at the theater where she was rehearsing. About Mrs. Grant herself —"

Helen Baxter had started working for her two years before. She was going to college at night and though she had managed to renew her scholarship each year — (I was right about the intelligence, Mr. Potter thought) — she still had to provide her own room and board. The job wasn't difficult. She added thoughtfully, "On the whole."

It was almost impossible to keep the place in order, but Mrs. Grant didn't seem to mind. Her chief responsibility was seeing that the clothes were pressed, mended and always ready to wear.

"Do you know anything about her friends?" O'Toole asked.

"I wasn't here in the evenings, Lieutenant. I could tell, of course, if she had had a party." She hesitated. "After all, the doorman will tell you, anyhow; there was someone who — didn't go home early."

"Men? Or man?"

She shrugged. "I don't know. You understand, all I have to go on are the telephone calls."

"Can you use names?" O'Toole asked.

"Not for the late-stayers. Recently, of course, she was seeing Mr. Thornton Grant chiefly. She told me she was going to marry him. He was here often in the late afternoon. It was all," the girl's lips quivered with amusement, "very decorous."

Mr. Potter asked, "What did you mean, Miss Baxter, when you said the job wasn't difficult 'on the whole'?"

She answered composedly. "One thing I must say for Mrs. Grant. She wasn't a very nice woman but she treated me with the same courtesy she would a white girl. That's not," she added dryly, "as usual as you might expect. Except — there were two terrific flareups: one because I answered the telephone while she was in her bath and she didn't want anyone to answer it but herself; the other time because the bedroom door was open while I was cleaning, she hadn't noticed it, and I overheard a scrap of the conversation. She — that day, she called me just about everything. And yet I didn't know what it was all about. She was wild."

"Angry, you mean?" O'Toole asked.

"No. She was terrified, that's why she blew me up. Over the telephone she kept saying, 'You've got to try again. That's all. You've got to find it.' Then she said, 'I know you

163

have, darling. But it isn't just on my account. You're in this, too.' "

"How long ago was this?"

"Three or four weeks, perhaps; anyhow, it was a couple of weeks after she told me she was going to marry Mr. Thornton Grant."

The telephone in the bedroom rang. A policeman grunted, "Yeah. Yeah." He waited. "Okay, I'll tell him."

He came to the door. "About those fingerprints they got here. Mrs. Grant's; her maid's — we had hers on record because of a robbery here a few weeks ago; some smears that look like gloves. And — Mallow's."

"Well," O'Toole said explosively. "Well! The lying —"

"I think —" the maid began.

"Well?"

"I think he came here only once. Just one of those things. After the rehearsals started. Maybe ten days ago. But I don't —"

"Go on," Mr. Potter said. "You make very good sense, young lady."

"Well, I don't think it mattered to either of them."

"What about the robbery?" O'Toole asked.

For the first time Helen Baxter was unsure. "I don't know," she admitted. "Personally, I think that Mrs. Grant faked it. One morning when I got here there were some pieces of jewelry missing, a diamond bracelet, a sapphire necklace. She never bothered to put her jewelry in a deposit box because she wanted it handy. Well, the dresser drawer was on the floor and the jewel box had been broken open. The insurance company was suspicious but they paid off. What puzzled them was that there was none of the usual publicity you get when an actress claims to be robbed. Especially when she's about to appear in a new play." She added rather grimly but surprisingly without bitterness, "Of course, they checked me from A to Z."

"You think she sold them?"

"I think," the maid said slowly, "she gave them to someone. She was simply furious but she was scared, too. She's been scared of something or someone ever since I started working here."

It was Mr. Potter who asked about the black dress. At his prompting she went carefully through the lavish wardrobe in the bedroom. At the back of the closet, hung out of sight, there was a simple black dress. She held it up. "I don't recognize this," she said. "It's new. She had a black dress but I don't see it here. She rarely wore black."

"Could she have given it away?" O'Toole asked.

165

"Not Mrs. Grant. She didn't give anything away. And I mean anything. If she was tired of it she'd have sold it."

"How long has the black dress been missing?"

"I pressed it yesterday. She asked me to."

"It looks," Mr. Potter commented, "as though Miss Grant had a point, as though the whole business of that ruined dress had been a plant to get her backstage."

"You can't have it two ways," O'Toole told him.

"Meaning?"

"If Eve cut up the dress herself, what was the limping man doing? I thought Miss Grant — and you — had him cast as the trouble-maker." When Mr. Potter remained silent, he turned back to the girl. "Do you know anything about Mrs. Grant's family?"

She gave him a swift look. "I know that her dresser, Mrs. Simmons, was her mother. Mrs. Grant sent for her when she began work on the play. I think she wanted a bodyguard, but she wanted one cheap."

She made a small angry gesture. "She lived like this and let her mother live — oh, just like a dog. I've got one room and we scrimp on food but my mother lives with me and we share."

★ ★ ★

"The more I learn about Eve Grant the less I like her," O'Toole commented as they climbed out of the police car at Mrs. Simmons' address on West End Avenue. It was a shabby run-down building, a walk-up. A policeman came to the car and shook his head. "All quiet."

"Gormer will relieve you," O'Toole told him. "I don't want her running around loose, at least not until she talks."

The one-room apartment was on the top floor at the back. What light filtered down the narrow shaft that separated it from a higher building was largely cut off by a heavy iron fire escape.

O'Toole's knock was followed by a hesitant voice calling, "Who is it?"

"Police."

Across the hall a door opened a crack while an interested neighbor listened. Mrs. Simmons opened the door. She had put on a shabby black dress, covered by an apron. Her hair was neatly arranged but her eyes were swollen and the lids were red. Without a word she stood back to let them come in.

"I don't know what more you want of me. I don't know anything about it."

The room contained a threadbare rug, a studio couch with sagging springs, an old rocking chair, and an upholstered chair with the stuffing oozing out of one arm. A screen failed to conceal a two-burner stove and a small sink where a tap was dripping, leaving rust. Sleazy curtains were tied back to admit the thin winter light.

"How'd you happen to take the job as your daughter's dresser?" O'Toole asked.

She hadn't expected the question. "Well, of course, I knew her ways; and then, I could use the money. She might as well pay me as anyone. She was giving me two hundred dollars a month."

"Your husband out of work?"

"Now my salary's cut off, he's out looking this morning. But Verne's got tuberculosis; that's why we was out in Arizona. Then when Allie — Eve — needed someone at the theater we came back here."

"Who was she afraid of?" O'Toole asked abruptly.

The woman stiffened in her chair. Her face tightened. She shook her head.

"There was someone," O'Toole insisted. "She said so herself."

"She never."

"She told Mr. Collinge about the telephone calls in the night and the troubles in her dressing room."

"I couldn't be there every minute," the

woman burst out. "Like I'd have to go to the john or use the pressing room or something like that."

"Who was it, Mrs. Simmons?"

"I don't know." She looked up at them, her eyes changing. "I heard the radio. You got Cass Grant. Isn't that enough?"

"Grant was in Wentworth while those other things were going on," O'Toole told her. "Day before yesterday, your daughter called the police."

"She never!" There was no mistaking the shock in the woman's face.

"When was the sleeve cut off that black dress?"

"Sometime during the first act, I guess," she said sullenly. "It was all right in the afternoon. Then I was standing in the wings, just for a little while, to watch Eve acting in that gorgeous white evening dress. A real star. And looking like an angel!" She swallowed, waited a moment. "Then when she come back to change — there it was, just slashed."

Mr. Potter looked at her, shaking his head. "It won't do, you know. We found her second-act costume at her apartment. The one that was cut up was an old one, wasn't it?"

The dresser made no reply but her lips pressed hard together.

"I think Eve cut that dress up herself, Mrs.

Simmons. For heaven's sake, tell us the truth about it! You're only making things tougher for yourself."

It was the urgency in his voice that made her change her tactics. "All right, I can't see it will hurt now. Eve wanted to get Miss Grant backstage. She had to. She couldn't think of any other way to do it."

"What did she want of her?"

"I don't know. She had some sort of plan. She was getting desperate, what with one thing and another. Only Miss Grant wouldn't stay. She musta gone as soon as I went out for the snaps. We couldn't have figured that in advance. I suppose, when it come to the point, Eve didn't know just how to handle it."

"How," Mr. Potter asked, "did she get that bruise on her arm?"

"I don't know."

"Look here, Mrs. Simmons, your daughter was afraid of someone and she wouldn't say who it was. So she died. I beg you to tell us what you know. The police will protect you in any way they can. But as long as you hold back information you are in danger. Do you understand?"

"I don't know anything," she said stubbornly.

"Last night," O'Toole reminded her, "you said you could still protect yourself."

"That's what I am doing. I didn't kill my girl. I've got trouble enough. Now get out."

Back in the police car, O'Toole told the driver to take them to the Plaza. The driver spoke without turning around. "Coupla items came through. Mallow's doctor checks his story. He often has to get treatments to take him through a performance. One of those incurable things. Only has a few years of active theater left, poor devil."

"Anything more?"

"Yeah. Eve Grant was born Allie Voss, daughter of Alfred and Sue Voss, on the Lower East Side, in nineteen forty-one. Voss died when she was seven. The mother married Verne Simmons in nineteen fifty-one. No war record. Has a tubercular condition. They moved to the Bronx. The girl dropped out of school at fifteen. Modeled for a Sixth Avenue — excuse me, Avenue of the Americas — wholesaler of underwear for a year. Then cigarette girl at a night club for a year. Then she was on her own. Seen around with Maitland Frederick."

"We're going to have to do a lot of digging," O'Toole grunted, "to find the men she played around with."

"She married Cass Grant in fifty-eight. Divorced him in fifty-nine after he was tried for murdering Frederick. His money had been

171

tied up by his father from the time of their marriage, so all she had in alimony was one hundred and fifty bucks a month. Since then, no known source of income except a couple of small walk-on parts on Broadway."

"We'll get to work on that income of hers," O'Toole said. "It's going to be the hell of a job. Everyone will clam up. But she got it somewhere. That apartment rents for six hundred and fifty dollars a month. Those furs alone could run to twelve or fifteen thousand. As for her jewelry — I wonder if she was blackmailing someone."

"It seems to have worked two ways," Mr. Potter pointed out. "That fake robbery, for instance; I don't see her handing over diamonds and sapphires for the fun of it."

O'Toole nodded. "She sure as hell wouldn't share the wealth if she could help it. Just two hundred dollars a month to her mother as a dresser, with the way she was loaded!"

Mr. Potter frowned. Mrs. Simmons wouldn't have done anything to hurt her daughter's chances. She certainly hadn't cashed in on Eve's first marriage; obviously she hadn't intended to let Thornton Grant know she was his prospective mother-in-law.

"I'll bet," Mr. Potter said savagely, "Eve never gave her mother a penny until she came to work for her. Did you see the woman's hands, man? I'll double anything you like that she has been working as a cleaning woman."

The doorman at the Plaza eyed the police car without favor. As the men began to pile out, he looked at the driver, who was in uniform.

"Look here," he began in alarm, "you can't —"

"I'm Lieutenant O'Toole, homicide. There won't be any trouble but we've got to talk to one of your guests. We'll be as quiet about it as we can."

"Homicide!" The doorman snapped his fingers for a bellhop who came running. "Call the manager, for God's sake. We've got the police here!"

TWELVE

Mrs. Frederick opened the door herself, her eyes widening as she saw the four men. Then she recognized Mr. Potter. In spite of her shock, she managed a faint smile.

"Somehow, I hadn't realized that this was bound to happen. Come in."

The living room had windows overlooking Central Park. It was comfortably but impersonally furnished except for three oil paintings on the walls, which Mr. Potter recognized at once as Fredericks.

He introduced O'Toole, Haskel and the sergeant. Mrs. Frederick sat down and motioned them to chairs. Her white hair was beautifully arranged, her simple wool dress finely cut and neutral, her manner had a gentle dignity. Her eyes followed Mr. Potter as he moved from canvas to canvas.

"How he could paint!" he exclaimed. "I've never seen any of these before. They must be youthful work. The brushwork is quite different."

"Maitland did them on our honeymoon. The ones that had not been sold at the time of his — his death went to his dealer. I — it seemed best to get rid of everything: the

174

furniture, the personal things, the paintings he did in his later years." Her voice was remote.

O'Toole let Mr. Potter take the lead. With a woman of this sort it would be more satisfactory.

"I suppose," Mr. Potter said, "you know why we are here, Mrs. Frederick."

"Eve Grant's murder last night." She lifted a handkerchief to lips where fine lines had begun to appear. "I saw the morning papers. A terrible thing. I have been greatly shocked."

She had nothing to add. After waiting a moment O'Toole said, "When did you leave the theater, Mrs. Frederick?"

"Oh, at once. Because Eve found my presence — disturbing. I walked home. I needed — I always need to walk when I have something to think out."

"In a snowstorm?"

She nodded. "I changed my shoes when I got home."

"How long did it take you to get here?"

"I don't really know," she said in surprise. "Twenty minutes. Perhaps twenty-five."

"Do you have a personal maid?"

"Only for a few hours in the morning. The hotel staff does the rest. But why — Oh, I see." She frowned as though making an effort to remember but she did not, Mr. Potter thought, seem to be alarmed. "There was the doorman, of course, but, as I recall, a party was leaving the hotel as I went in and he was opening the door of a taxi for them. The elevator operator — but I'm under the impression that the elevator was nearly filled."

"You aren't sure then that anyone could vouch for the time when you came back here."

"But," she stopped, turned to Mr. Potter, "surely the police can't conceivably suspect that I killed Eve Grant. It's preposterous. What possible reason could I have had?"

"She had an affair with your husband," O'Toole reminded her bluntly.

Mrs. Frederick was impatient. "My good man, that was four years ago! And Maitland is gone. There is no," her voice was tinged with irony, "rivalry to combat. In any case, my husband had been notoriously unfaithful to me for years. Eventually we worked out an impersonal sort of relationship. He remained a delightful and stimulating companion; as long as he left me any vestige of dignity, we maintained a marriage of sorts."

She flushed as she realized that the sergeant was recording her words. "Maitland did not want a divorce. Marriage was his," again the irony, "protection against any enduring entanglement. No woman could hold his interest for long. He had always been," she groped for words, "reasonably discreet. But Eve was so exquisitely beautiful that she appealed to the painter as well as to the man. She really got under his skin. He lost his head. That's why he took a lease on the house next door to the Grants. But he didn't want to marry the girl. He was terribly upset when I told him that morning I'd divorce him unless it stopped, that he could not conduct an affair practically in my own house; it was too gross an insult. That — never. After I found the picture, he gave me his word that it was over for him."

"And you believed him?" O'Toole asked.

"I never knew Maitland to break his word," she said

Mr. Potter leaned forward. "When did this conversation with your husband take place?"

"Just before he died. Perhaps a half hour, more or less." She twisted her hands together, her face drawn with anguish. "If I had only waited to talk to him before I called the Grants! O God, if I had only waited! All these years I've known that I was to blame. But I'd gone to the studio and I'd seen that picture of Eve. By the time I'd talked to Janet, it was too late. Maitland came home and promised to break with Eve and went out to the studio. Before I could call Janet back, Thornton came and then Cass! So Maitland had to die and Cass must have wanted to die and Janet changed. She's not the same girl any more. Only Eve continued to flourish, like one of those poisonous trees that destroy the life around it."

She looked at the men who watched her. "I'm not going to say I'm sorry that Eve is dead. She was evil. The only person I'm sorry for is the one who was driven to killing her last night."

"Why," O'Toole asked, "did you lie at the trial, Mrs. Frederick? Under oath you testified that there was no picture of Eve Grant."

"Because I knew that picture gave Cass a terrific motive and I was so dreadfully sorry for him."

"You believe he killed your husband?"

She looked at him in what appeared to be genuine astonishment. "But there was no question about it! I warned Janet not to have him released, that he was dangerous."

"Now that your cards are all on the table," Mr. Potter said noncommittally, and O'Toole shot him a quick look, "will you tell us what really did happen when your husband was killed?"

She had gone out to the studio, while Maitland was away, to see for herself the picture he was painting of Eve. She had promptly tried to get in touch with Cass Grant but couldn't reach him. Instead, she had got Janet and issued her warning. Maitland had come home and she had given her ultimatum. Unless he broke with Eve, completely and at once, she would divorce him and name Eve. Maitland had agreed.

"He was considerably upset," she added dryly. "He went out to the studio. Then Thornton Grant came. He insisted on seeing Maitland and he went out to the studio. He came back within three or four minutes. He said he had knocked several times but Maitland would not open the door, although he was moving around in there."

The color faded from her face. "Then — Cass came. He went through the house like a cyclone. Thornton was talking to me in the drawing room and tried to stop him. Cass simply shoved him out of the way. It was nearly fifteen minutes before he came back. He looked like a dead man. He said he had found Maitland's body. He had been strangled."

She was silent, drained of emotion, exhausted.

"And then?" Mr. Potter said at last, his voice quiet.

She lifted a hand, let it drop again. "Then it all started — the police, the questioning, the crowds outside the house, the headlines, the horror."

"Who called the police?"

"Thornton, after he'd run out to the studio to see for himself. He came back and looked at Cass, who simply stood there. I don't believe he knew where he was. He was in a state of shock. Thornton said, 'You criminal fool!' and he called the police. Cass didn't say anything. He just stood. Then Thornton grabbed his arm and said, 'You're to wait here,' as though Cass were trying to escape. And Cass said in the strangest, emptiest tone, 'Why? There's nothing left to wait for. Ever. Nothing at all.'"

At O'Toole's request she started as though she had come back from a great distance. Yes, of course, they could see the clothes she had worn the night before. Without interest, she called her maid who, bright-eyed with curiosity, got them out: dress, coat, gloves, shoes, underclothing. She'd rinsed out the stockings, she admitted. Haskel told her that it didn't matter. He went to work but found no trace of fluoroscin. Mrs. Frederick held out her hands indifferently. They, too, showed no trace of the plant.

O'Toole reached for his hat, raised his brows at Mr. Potter.

"There are a couple of questions," Mr. Potter said. "That window cleaner Miss Grant saw —"

"We hadn't hired a window cleaner," Mrs. Frederick said. "Janet, poor dear, was trying to protect Cass."

"But she didn't," Mr. Potter pointed out, "suggest the man had killed your husband, you know. She claimed only that he saw the murder, that he afterwards entered the Grants' house. She saw him coming along a garden path. She heard the step of a limping man in Mrs. Grant's bedroom. She thought he was the one who struck Mrs. Grant. If you remember, Mrs. Grant's face was badly bruised when the police saw her on the day of your husband's murder. She said then that Cass had struck her just before he set off to kill Mr. Frederick. Later, at the trial, she reversed herself but no one believed her then, of course. Presumably she was protecting him."

"Even if there were any such man," Mrs. Frederick said, "I never saw him. Of course, if he was working on the skylight he wouldn't have been visible from our house. The skylight is on the other side."

"Is there any way the limping man — or anyone — could have reached the studio without going through either house?"

"Well, as you probably know, the houses

are joined together. They take up the whole frontage on the street. The studio was at the rear of the property, halfway between the two houses, and back of that were the buildings on Sixty-seventh Street, which have been built since the twin houses were constructed. Unless someone were to go through the basement of one of them, or a window, I honestly don't know."

O'Toole nodded to Haskel; the sergeant pocketed his notebook and stood up. Then Mr. Potter asked another question.

"What made all of you so sure that Thornton Grant never entered the studio?"

"But," Mrs. Frederick said blankly, "he said so. And he heard Maitland inside."

"How do you know?"

Mrs. Frederick recovered from her stunned surprise. For the first time she managed a real smile. "Thornton! That's incredible. There's no reason on earth. He wasn't involved in any possible way with Maitland, the merest acquaintance; and he certainly couldn't have been involved with Eve. Not Thornton."

"He was planning to marry her three weeks from today," Mr. Potter said. "It would be interesting to know when he first fell in love with her."

"Thornton and Eve." Mrs. Frederick laughed. "I wouldn't have believed even Eve could produce such a miracle."

"By the way," Mr. Potter asked, "do you still have your key to the house?"

She shook her head. "When I gave the place up they were turned over to Thornton Grant."

"Thornton comes next," O'Toole said, after he had sent Haskel back to headquarters. "How well do you know him?"

"Now and then we meet at a club. We've played bridge together three or four times. The merest acquaintance."

"How serious were you when you made that crack about him?"

"I don't know," Mr. Potter admitted. "But there are some factors: we know now he was interested in Eve, we know Cass's father had practically cut of his son's income; it's more than likely he told Thornton the money would eventually come into his hands unless Cass made something of himself. Thornton doesn't seem to have any alibi. People took his word for what happened at the Frederick murder."

"He was certainly never seriously considered," O'Toole agreed thoughtfully. "The man radiates a kind of malignant probity. And, of course, there was Cass."

"There was Cass," Mr. Potter agreed, "a sitting duck if there ever was one. By the way, can you get me in to see him?"

"Why don't you ask Russlin to arrange it?"

"I like being direct when I can."

O'Toole gave him an affectionate grin. "And when you can't?"

"Then I have to be devious," Mr. Potter said cheerfully.

The houseman who admitted them to Thornton's house had all the decorous gloom of the head of a funeral parlor. It was some time before Thornton came down the stairs. Mr. Potter was appalled by the change in him. His cheeks seemed to have fallen in, his eyes were sunken, his head had acquired a nervous tic, jerking to the right. However, he held himself erect and he spoke quietly.

"Good morning, gentlemen. Sit down, won't you? Sorry to keep you waiting. I've been trying," his voice broke and he steadied it, "to find out when I can make arrangements for Eve — for the services."

"The autopsy will be completed today," O'Toole said. "The body will probably be released tomorrow morning."

"Thank you." Thornton had regained his self-control. "Now what can I do to help?"

Somewhat to his surprise, O'Toole did not refer to the murder of Eve. Instead, he took him step by step through the discovery of Maitland Frederick's body, four years ago. Thornton answered readily, his story exactly the same as the one he had told at the trial. While he talked, Mr. Potter drifted idly around the room and out to the kitchen. In the butler's pantry beyond, the servant was telephoning a grocery order.

Mr. Potter looked around quickly. In a closed cupboard under the sink he found what he was looking for, covered garbage cans. Quietly he eased the top off one and peered in, his nostrils flaring in distaste. He closed it in a hurry, opened the other, which was filled with papers. He felt down among them, pulled out a paperback book, Ovid's *Metamorphoses*, translated by Horace Gregory.

As the servant appeared, he closed the can and the cupboard door. "A glass of water, please," he said. He dropped the book into his pocket, aware that the man's suspicious eyes were on it. He sipped the water, set down the glass, and strolled back.

Thornton was still talking. ". . . so after I had taken a look in the studio to be sure that it was actually true, I went to the house to telephone the police. And I didn't let Cass make a break for it."

"Did he try to make a break for it?" Mr. Potter sounded interested.

Thornton hesitated.

"We've just been talking with Mrs. Frederick," Mr. Potter informed him.

185

"Oh. Well, no telling what he might have done. I didn't give him the opportunity."

"I'll admit," Mr. Potter said, "I was surprised by the card left on Mrs. Grant's body. Somehow, I wouldn't have thought your cousin was a reader of the classics."

Thornton took his time lighting a cigarette. "It was a classical quotation?"

"*The Metamorphoses*," O'Toole said. "I gathered from Mr. Potter that the classics are your field."

Thornton looked amused. "No man could be familiar with every line. And for the past two years I've paid little attention to Latin. I've been concentrating on a study of the revenge motif as it runs through the Greek drama."

"Do you have a copy of the Gregory translation of Ovid?" O'Toole asked.

"You are quite free to examine my library. It's on the second floor. But please be most careful in handling the books and manuscripts I have behind glass. Some of them are irreplaceable."

As O'Toole got up, Mr. Potter reached in his pocket, laid the paperback book on the table.

"It isn't necessary," he said. "This was in a garbage can in the kitchen." He looked steadily at Thornton. "Sorry I had to do it this way, but I felt pretty sure you'd dispose of it as quickly as possible."

There were red flecks in Thornton's eyes. The anger that consumed him was like a fire burning the man's guts. Half a minute passed before he as able to speak, and even then his voice was shaking.

"Don't you find scavenging rather a dirty job, Potter?"

"Very. But cleaner, perhaps, than murder. Cleaner, perhaps, even than revenge."

Thornton was under control now. "Naturally I recognized the quotation. In the circumstances, I'd have been a fool to keep the book around."

"Suppose," O'Toole said, "we go over your movements last night, Mr. Grant. You claimed that you spent the intermission in the lobby, smoking. So did your cousin. Sanders Newton was telephoning in the lobby — we've checked that — and he didn't see either of you."

Thornton's head jerked, the new habit it had acquired. "I tried to talk to Cass but he turned on his heel and went out. You know as well as I do where he went. Along the alley to the fire escape and to Eve's room where, with or without Janet's connivance, he killed her. You arrested him. What more do you want, in God's name?"

"We are holding him for questioning,"

O'Toole corrected him.

"By the way," Mr. Potter said, "I understand you tried to persuade Cass to leave the country. Why?"

"To prevent another tragedy," Thornton answered promptly. "I warned Janet that it wasn't safe to release him."

"It wasn't to make sure Cass was out of the country before you married Eve?"

Thornton made no reply. O'Toole took up his questions. "Now — about your own movements last night, Mr. Grant."

"If you are going to question me further, I'll call my lawyer."

Mr. Potter spoke abruptly. "If Cass should be indicted again, do you intend to turn over his money to finance the trial?"

"And help him escape the electric chair a second time? I couldn't justify that to my own conscience. It would be like setting a panther free to prowl through the streets of a crowded city. I warned Janet to leave him where he was. I told her he was dangerous. If she wants to finance a new trial, she has her own money. I turned it all over to her several months ago."

"Why?" Mr. Potter demanded.

"Why don't you ask her?" Thornton got up, his air of decision, of dignity, of authority, marred by the horrible little tic that jerked his head. "You can arrest me or you can get

188

out of here. But I've said my last word except in the presence of my lawyer."

The men got up. Mr. Potter handed O'Toole the paperback book.

"You should have tried the fireplace," he told Thornton gently. "Paper burns so much more easily than canvas."

Before the police car drove off, Mr. Potter said, "Don't forget to get me in to see Cass Grant."

He hailed a cab and gave Collinge's address. Collinge was still asleep, the harassed servant told him, and the phone had been ringing all morning. It rang again.

"For you, sir."

At first Mr. Potter could distinguish nothing in the babble of sound. "Speak more slowly."

"Mr. Potter, it's Janet Grant. For God's sake, come!"

"Where? Your house?"

"No." She described a dairy lunch on Fourth Street. "Please hurry! Please! He's been strangled!"

"Who has?"

There was a click as the connection was broken off.

THIRTEEN

At ten o'clock that morning, Janet opened her eyes and looked automatically at her bedside clock. After Pete's telephone call the night before, telling her that Cass was being held for questioning, she had been unable to sleep. Even Pete would be unable to save him a second time.

It was all going to happen again — the questioning, the ugly notoriety, a trial. Cass behind bars. Cass, this time, in the death house. She was cold with horror. If she had only left him at Wentworth! Everyone had warned her: Mrs. Frederick, Thornton, Pete himself.

Little by little, she had curbed her panic, tried to think constructively. Grants didn't give up so easily. Cass wasn't guilty. He hadn't killed Maitland Frederick or Eve. He had had only one purpose: to clear his name, to find out who the killer was. That was what she had to cling to, the knowledge that the killer existed, that he had to be found.

Only — how could she go about it? In the library she picked up the big Manhattan telephone directory in its heavy leather case, looked up Graham Collinge's number. Mr.

Potter would know what to do. Hiram Potter —

She let the directory slip out of her hands. He had believed her. Well, hadn't he? And he had turned to her, like flame consuming gunpowder; there had been a moment of liquid fire, and then he had gone away. He hadn't expected that to happen. He hadn't wanted it to happen. But that quiet man with the smooth fair hair had made her feel more alive than she had ever been, more aware of herself. He was an anchor in a storm, a shield against the beastliness that lay ahead. But he was also a catalytic agent. One minute in his arms had wiped out the memory, the comfort of Pete's steady, fortifying affection. And Pete had sacrificed his profession, his future for her, for Cass.

I don't care, she told herself defiantly. Not even for gratitude, not even for Cass, not even to pay the debt we owe Pete will I let this thing go. When you find the best, you cling to it.

It was late when she went wearily up the stairs to bed, her body depleted, her mind wide-awake. She took a sleeping pill and at last plunged into heavy sleep.

The heaviness still hung over her in the morning. She stared dully at the clock. Ten! The maid was supposed to bring coffee at eight. She had probably been too deeply asleep to hear the knock. She rang the bell over the bed and sat up.

In a few moments the maid appeared with coffee on a tray. She wore street clothes and a hat. As she put the tray on Janet's knees she avoided her eyes, closed the window and spoke without looking at her.

"I'm sorry, Miss, but we saw the morning papers. We're — well, we're going. The other servants left half an hour ago. I thought one of us ought to stay to tell you why. Now — you can see how it is. We'll have trouble getting other jobs if we're mixed up in — anything. You," she ended lamely, "can see how it is."

"Yes, I can see."

The maid went out, closing the door quietly behind her. Janet drank the coffee and then bathed and dressed, brushing the pale hair severely back from her face, noticing that the shadows under her eyes made them bigger, darker than usual. The effect was melodramatic but there was nothing she could do about it.

Her footsteps sounded loud in the empty house as she went down the stairs. She'd get breakfast on her way to the shop. In the front hall she heard the sounds for the first time, peered out cautiously. A crowd had gathered, newsmen and cameramen easily distinguishable among the curiosity-seekers.

She drew back. She couldn't face them. Not now. She telephoned the shop to say she wouldn't be in for a few days, gave hurried instructions.

"We'll manage here," the head saleswoman assured her. "And try not to worry too much, Miss Lord." She added cynically, "At least, the publicity has brought in a lot of customers."

In the kitchen Janet made toast and poured another cup of coffee. With the house besieged, she could not leave it but she could not endure inaction. She had better call Pete and find out where Cass was, when she could see him.

Before she could dial his office number, her telephone rang. The voice was one she had never heard before, a man's hoarse voice.

"Miss Grant?"

"This is Miss Grant."

"It's time we had a little talk."

"Who are you?" she asked sharply.

He chuckled. "You ought to know. You've been talking about me long enough. Four years, isn't it? And last night I saw you in the alley."

"Who are you?"

"In fact, we nearly met."

"The limping man!"

"Now look." The hoarse voice was brisk. "We haven't got a lot of time. Get this straight the first round. Way things are, they aren't going to let your brother off again. Unless we can make a little arrangement, he's had it."

"What kind of arrangement?"

"Well, this is how it is. I saw the murder of Frederick."

"And Eve?"

Again the chuckle. "You expect a lot. Nope, I didn't see that one, but it don't matter. I know who did it. You weren't the only one backstage last night." He gave a kind of gasp that was sheer rage. "Walking like me. Going to pin it on me. I mighta known." The voice became businesslike. "Now, Miss Grant, I can clear your brother but I expect it to be worth my while, what with the chances I am taking, and believe me there are plenty. Get it?"

"Yes, of course. I'll do anything, anything you say."

"I want fifty thousand dollars. Cash on the line. And I want it today. Then I'll tell you how Frederick died and why Eve died. But get this clear — you tell anyone about this call before I get the money and the deal's off. I gotta get away first. See? This is strictly a one-time offer, lady."

"Fifty thousand dollars," Janet repeated slowly.

The hoarse voice roughened. "Don't tell me you haven't got it. I know your cousin turned it over to you, all your own money."

"But not in cash. I'd have to sell securities. It can't be done in a day; it would take time. And the bank would be curious, especially now."

"That's your lookout. Borrow it if you have to; you're good for that much money. It's that or the chair for your brother. That simple. Tell 'em you need cash on the line for your brother's defense."

"Oh, the government bonds," Janet exclaimed. "I have twenty-five thousand in government bonds. And I can take some out of the shop account. I — all right —"

He gave her instructions. There was an abandoned warehouse on Seventh Avenue in the Village. He'd be waiting for her. She was to have the money in small bills not marked or numbered in sequence. She was to come alone. She was to confide in no one or he'd never open his mouth. Clear?

It was clear but —

The telephone clicked and Janet stared at it. The limping man! Hope surged through her. At last he was going to talk. At an abandoned warehouse. Abandoned. Anyone could have made that telephone call. Anyone at all. She'd be a fool to meet a strange man with no one to protect her, with fifty thousand dollars in her possession. But suppose he really was the limping man, suppose he could save Cass?

She paced up and down the floor, her clasped hands pressed to her lips in an agony of indecision. Then she dialed Pete's office. The receptionist's voice sharpened with curiosity when she identified herself. She conferred with Pete's secretary. Mr. Russlin was in court. He'd be back before lunch because he had an appointment with a client. He'd call Miss Grant at once. Yes, she understood the matter was urgent.

Janet reached blindly for the Manhattan directory, called Graham Collinge's number. Her heart was pounding erratically. The servant at the end of the line was sorry. Mr. Potter had gone out very early, before breakfast. He'd left no instructions. When he came back? Miss Janet Grant? Urgent? Yes, madam.

She put down the telephone, feeling empty, abandoned, as though he should have been there when she needed him. In the small room that had been her mother's morning room she sat down at the desk and got out checkbooks. She could withdraw twelve thousand from the shop account, temporarily at least; five thousand from savings. She hunted for the key to her safety deposit box. She could cash in her government bonds. It didn't add up to enough. There was about five thousand in her personal checking account, but she couldn't draw it all out.

She scrawled meaningless hieroglyphics on a pad, bit the end of her pen. What else? She couldn't borrow from Pete who was always broke. Thornton? She shook her head. He wouldn't lift a finger. He hated Cass. Perhaps he always had. Undoubtedly he had from the time when Cass married Eve. Was that, she wondered, when he had fallen in love with her?

She could sell the two houses, but that would take weeks, more like months. There was her mother's pearl necklace in the safety deposit box. Not that! Yes, why not, if it would save Cass?

She ran back to her room, chose a hat, was adjusting it in front of the mirror when she remembered the mob outside the house. How was she going to get out? In the storage room on the third floor she found an old straw suitcase left behind by a servant many years ago. Out of a trunk that smelled of mothballs she pulled an odd-shaped cape, almost like a serape, which her grandmother had once bought in Europe and had insisted on wearing over the protests and laughter of her family. It was warm and comfortable, she had maintained, being a stout individualist, and that was all that mattered. She found a wool scarf to tie around her head, concealing her fair hair.

In the bedroom she put them on, added dark glasses, picked up the straw suitcase and went down to the basement. Before opening the outside door onto the areaway, she took a long breath and then went out, hearing the safety catch click behind her. She gave the mob a surly look and pushed her way through them, heading toward Madison Avenue.

After a first quick glance, the mob lost interest. Just another servant quitting her job. Detective Milstein, who had mingled casually with the crowd, followed her with his eyes, thinking that you didn't often see such a dowdy-looking maid in a high-class establishment as the Grants'. Did a double-take. Those high heeled shoes were like the ones his wife had looked at in a Fifth Avenue window. Made in Italy, she said, and cheap at sixty dollars. That queer-looking cape had reeked of mothballs. The dark glasses —

He set off briskly toward Madison, saw a taxi stop, broke into a run.

In the woman's room at Grand Central Station Janet took off the cape and scarf, opened the suitcase and slid her arms into the fur coat she had packed in it. She pulled a small beret of matching fur over her fair hair and set the suitcase down against the wall.

At the bank the teller gave her a quick searching look and then began counting out money. "This is too much for you to carry safely, Miss Grant."

"It's a cash deal and someone is waiting for me outside," she said. "Anyhow, I won't be carrying it more than a few minutes."

It made a bigger package than she had expected and she had difficulty in stuffing it into her large handbag.

The teller's eyes followed her as she went toward the vault.

She waited impatiently for her safety deposit box. Because her hand was shaking she had trouble opening it. From the case that contained her mother's pearls, she drew the necklace out, touched it gently, and then dropped it, too, into the handbag. The government bonds she gathered up and took to the desk.

"I want to cash these in."

This clerk, too, had read the papers. He gave her the swift, appraising look to which she had become accustomed, to which she had never become reconciled.

"Some unexpected emergency," she said

hastily, knowing that she should not attempt to explain, unable to stop herself.

He looked at her again, a look with none of the admiration most men gave her; indeed, without a trace of friendliness.

For heaven's sake, she thought, he believes I killed Eve. He thinks I'm trying to make a getaway. Laughter rose in her throat, then a wave of sickness. At her request, the money was placed in envelopes held together by a heavy rubber band.

"That's not safe," he told her in disapproval. "You're just asking for trouble."

She pushed back her chair and stood up. "It will be all right." As she walked swiftly back through the bank, she saw the teller who had cashed her checks in conversation with a man whose back was turned. He looked up, said something to the man, who swung around. Janet felt her cheeks burning. The murderer's sister. Perhaps, even, the murderer. She went through the revolving doors, signaled a taxi that had just pulled in to the curb to discharge a passenger, gave the Village address. She sat erect, clutching her handbag and the thick bunch of envelopes. She did not look back.

Behind her, Detective Milstein was saying to the driver of his cab, "Just don't lose sight of her, that's all."

"Hey, is there going to be any shooting?" the cabbie asked in alarm.

"No shooting," Milstein assured him.

"She run out on you?"

"She's running out on the law." Milstein added carefully, for he was a just man, "At least, it looks like it."

Next to the deserted warehouse, a crumbling building with broken windows, there was, fortunately, a shabby tenement.

"This is the place," Janet said.

"That's not the number you gave me."

"I got mixed up." She looked at the meter, paid him, and stepped into the filthy entrance of the tenement. It smelled of cabbage and garlic and, worse, of primitive and inadequate plumbing. A baby carriage took up most of the space.

As soon as the taxi had driven off, Janet went out quickly. She took a swift look around her. At a window across the street an elderly woman in a wheel chair had pulled back dirty curtains to have an unimpeded view of her neighbors. Down the street a man had got out of a taxi and was apparently arguing about the price that showed on the meter.

She walked to the warehouse. Tentatively she tried the door, which opened at her touch. She went in and closed it behind her. The main floor was in a state of dilapidation. Odds

201

and ends of lumber, broken pieces of plaster, shards of glass, old packing boxes. There was no light except for the small amount that filtered through the filthy windows. The place smelled of dampness and rotting vegetables and mice.

She stood still, listening. Perhaps he hadn't come yet. The floor boards were broken, with big splinters. Somewhere there was a creaking sound. A kind of echo. On the second floor? The stairs were at the right. At some time the railing had been ripped off.

A scrabbling sound. Rats! Wide-eyed, she looked around her, her heart pounding. There was a footstep overhead. She started toward the stairs. Stopped. Suppose someone else was up there, a tramp taking refuge from the winter cold. Someone who — appalling pictures flashed through her mind of sex maniacs.

The steps again. Halting steps. Familiar steps. The limping man was upstairs.

"Hello," she shouted. "You, up there!"

There was a startled exclamation, then queer sounds she, couldn't recognize at all. Then someone seemed to be pounding on the floor, drumming with his heels. Then footsteps again. Running steps. But these had no halt in them, they were strong and even. A window crashed. Silence.

"Hello!" she called again.

Cautiously, staying close to the wall she climbed the steep stairs. It was darker up here. The same clutter. The tiny scurry that was a mouse.

"Where are you?" she called, fear making her voice high and shrill.

At the back, a window was wide open on the rusty fire escape and a bitter wind came in. That must have been the sound she heard, someone opening the window; someone, then, who wasn't the limping man. But he had been there; she could not mistake the rhythm of his halting step.

There wasn't a sound except for a slithering in the wall that made her shiver. She was alone up here. If she had been afraid of what she might find, it was slight compared with the fear that she would find nobody, that Cass's one hope was gone.

"I'm leaving now," she said, her voice loud and clear. "I brought — it with me but, if you don't come at once, I'll take it back."

No one. Nothing. She turned toward the stairs, went back to look behind a pile of packing boxes.

She didn't faint. When the blackness receded she was holding herself upright against the boxes, looking at the man crumpled on the floor behind them. He had a long drooping nose. He had one eyebrow higher than the other. He had a noose embedded in his throat.

FOURTEEN

There was a neon light in the window of the dairy lunch. Janet sat on a stool at the counter, an untouched cup of coffee in front of her. She was drained of color and shaken by a tremor.

After a quick look at her, Mr. Potter slid onto the stool beside her. The only other customers were a party of four in a booth at the back, exchanging noisy banter with the proprietor, who was propped against the side of the booth, laughing. None of them paid any attention to the white-faced girl.

"Are you all right?" Mr. Potter asked.

It was a moment before the big eyes focused on him. The tremor that shook her body increased.

"You aren't going to faint, are you?"

She shook her head. Then her hand groped for his wrist, fastened on it. "He was strangled. Almost before my eyes. I even heard it. The way his feet kept drumming. He must have fought to live." She clamped her jaws tight to stop the chattering of her teeth.

Mr. Potter touched her coffee cup. It was almost cold. He started to call the proprietor. Better not. He would be bound to notice

Janet's overwrought condition, to be curious, to remember.

"Tell me as quickly as you can."

She made an effort to regain control and then started with the telephone call from the limping man, her attempts to reach Pete Russlin and him, her escape from the house in disguise, collecting the money, and her arrival at the warehouse.

She had certainly left a trail a mile wide, he thought, his heart sinking.

"Whoever did it," she concluded, "heard me call out. He threw up a window and got away down the fire escape. And the limping man is dead. There's no one now who can clear Cass."

She caught her breath, her fingers dug into his arm. "I hadn't realized — I was so dazed — but this really helps Cass, doesn't it? Because he couldn't have killed that man."

She saw Mr. Potter's expression then, broke off, her fingers released their frenzied grasp on his arm, crept up to her throat. "Oh. People will think I did it to help him, because he had an alibi, or because the limping man was blackmailing me. O God!"

"Steady. I can't have you going to pieces. You've got to keep your wits about you." He looked dubiously at the long black eyes. "I'm counting on you to help me, Janet."

Slowly the expression that so disturbed him diminished. She was able to take in what he said. "You're still going to help Cass, aren't you?"

"We're both going to help him," he answered her. "But you've got to be under full control. Now I want you to go home. I'll be in touch with you later on, as soon as I can. Wait for my call and trust me."

"Oh, I do. I do." She slid off the stool. She held herself erect with a visible effort. "What happens now?"

"I'll call the police." A moment's pause. "It hadn't occurred to you to do that?"

"The police," she said bitterly, "have not done much for my family."

He found a cab for her, warned her to be careful of the money she was carrying, and went back to the dairy lunch where he entered the telephone booth and called O'Toole.

"I was just leaving," the lieutenant told him. "The man we had watching the Grant girl called in. He found the body. We'll pick you up."

Mr. Potter waited on the street for the official car. As they drove around the corner to the warehouse, he repeated Janet's story.

"Did you get a look at the body?" O'Toole asked.

"I haven't been inside the building. We met

207

at that dairy lunch place where I called you."

"Milstein did. Soon as he realized the girl was disguised he tailed her to Grand Central where she changed her clothes. If he hadn't seen her pictures in the paper, he'd have lost her when she came out of the women's room. He followed her to the bank where she practically cleaned out her accounts and then she went down to the vault, then to the warehouse. He saw her go in. She was there maybe ten minutes, and then she shot out of the place like a bat out of hell. He saw her go to the lunchroom, telephone and sit down to wait so he went back to take a look. You knew the guy was strangled?"

Mr. Potter nodded.

"She's no fool, that girl," O'Toole said unexpectedly. "First she sees a limping man. Then he dies. Then she claims there's another limping man!"

Mr. Potter was silent. There wasn't, at the moment, anything he could say to answer the cold challenge in O'Toole's voice.

Men were already climbing out of official cars in front of the warehouse by the time O'Toole's car was parked. Mr. Potter kept out of the way while they went efficiently about their jobs. He looked up and down the street. The warehouse took up most of the block on one side, with a vacant lot at one end and at the other an old tenement. On the other side of the street there were tenement buildings, several of which had one-room newsstand-candy shops on the first floor, where cigarettes could be bought, one or two at a time.

On the second floor of a building nearly across the street from the warehouse, an old woman was peering out from behind parted curtains. Mr. Potter hoped she had been sitting there for the past half hour and had not just been attracted by the sirens. She might have seen something useful.

While the photographers and fingerprint men worked, he paced the floor, deep in thought. If the limping man's story were true, if he had been a witness to the Frederick murder, he had, presumably, been blackmailing the killer for four years. Why had he changed his tactics now? And how had he known that Janet had regained her own fortune? That story had not appeared in the press. There was only one way he could see in which he could have acquired that information.

O'Toole called from the head of the stairs and Mr. Potter went up to join the group of men who stood looking down on the quiet body. The medical examiner got up, brushed off his knees.

"The poor devil was crippled, probably had

tuberculosis of the bones. He hasn't been dead much more than thirty minutes."

O'Toole looked at Mr. Potter. "Ever see him before?"

Mr. Potter shook his head.

"No identification on him. We'll check his fingerprints."

"Why," Mr. Potter suggested, "don't you have Haskel go over him?"

"Fluoroscin? You still believe the Grant girl, don't you?"

"Yes, I believe her. And, O'Toole — why don't you get Mrs. Simmons down here to see whether she can identify him?"

O'Toole gave him a long look. "You think he's the stepfather?"

"He knew Miss Grant had control of her own money. The only way I can see that he could possibly have known that is the link from Thornton Grant to Eve to the limping man."

"Why?"

"Why did Eve tell him? I don't know. It seems a possibility, that's all."

Three-quarters of an hour later, Haskel called O'Toole's office. The latter spoke briefly, turned to Mr. Potter.

"All right, so your hunch paid off. There was fluoroscin on the back of his coat and on his hands."

"At least, Miss Grant's story checks so far," Mr. Potter said. "She heard him in the alley, she touched the back of his coat. I think we can assume, then, that she was telling the truth about his connection with the first murder."

A policeman appeared in the doorway, stood aside to let Mrs. Simmons pass him. She wore a shabby old cloth coat that was inadequate protection against the January winds, and a wool scarf wrapped around her head. Remembering Eve's furs, Mr. Potter felt a twinge of anger against the dead girl.

O'Toole evidently shared his feeling for, in spite of the annoyance he had felt last time he saw her, he was gentle with her. There was someone they wanted her to see. It would take only a moment. Apathetically she accompanied them. For a long moment she stared down at the body of the dead man, while a watchful O'Toole held her arm to support her in case of collapse.

"That's Verne," she said at last, her voice unexpectedly loud. "That's him. My husband."

She began to laugh, wild hysterical laughter. O'Toole's hand tightened on her arm. He pushed her into a chair. She laughed on and on, gasped finally to a stop. She wiped her eyes.

"He's dead." Her voice was hoarse. "He's dead."

"I'm sorry we had to let you know in this sudden way. We should have prepared you."

"Sorry? I'm not sorry. I'm glad. I'm glad! I've never got to be afraid of him again as long as I live. I can't hardly believe it."

At Mr. Potter's suggestion, the two men took the unreluctant widow to lunch. She ate voraciously, as though she had been undernourished for a long time, and she talked incessantly, words pouring out in a steady stream. Later, an exhausted O'Toole said it had reminded him of a cork blowing out of a bottle of charged water.

"We was always scared of him, me and Eve. He had a real nasty temper and he knocked us around. He sold her to Frederick when she was no more'n seventeen. Well, I guess Eve didn't mind so much. I guess Frederick was quite a man at that and Eve was all woman. He was crazy about her, and he give Verne money now and then. But, acourse, she had to marry. She had her future to think of. In her way, Eve was real smart. Frederick knew she had to marry someone and I guess he thought it wouldn't make so much difference in the long run."

Something like a leer on her face sickened the two men. "I guess it didn't, at that. When she married, Eve give me money to go away. I wouldn't of fit in with the Grants. I got a job, cleaning woman in an office building in Arizona. I guess Eve hoped Verne would go, too. He's got — I mean he had tuberculosis. But after all that talk about the limping man, I didn't dare say that. It was his bones."

"Your husband didn't go with you?"

"No, he stayed around here. Where the money was. Trust Verne for that."

"Where did he get it, Mrs. Simmons?"

She shrugged. "Sometimes Frederick. Sometimes Eve. But she didn't have much of anything while she was married to Cass Grant. Her father-in-law didn't like the marriage a bit and he made Cass work for what he had. Then, afterwards, of course, he made a settlement on her so's she'd testify for Cass. Three hundred thousand dollars he gave her. But that was after Frederick painted the picture and his wife saw it and all the trouble began."

"Did you ever see that picture yourself, Mrs. Simmons?" O'Toole asked.

For the first time the avalanche of words was checked. Then she shrugged her bony shoulders. "I guess it don't matter now, and there's been enough harm done. Too much harm done. Yeah, Verne always kept close touch with Alli — Eve. He knew she and

Frederick had gone on — meeting, you know? He figured they were up to something and he kept a close watch on that studio after she started going there. Once he got in and took a picture of that painting Frederick was doing of her."

She didn't look up. The horrible greed with which she had wolfed down her food was momentarily appeased. There was a dull flush on her cheekbones. "I don't see how she could of. I brought her up real nice. Always the lady. Acourse, he was tickled pink. Frederick paid up and no questions asked when he asked him to buy the negative. Only Verne had already made prints."

"How many?" Mr. Potter asked.

"Four. One for him, one for Frederick, one for Eve, one — I just don't know and that's a fact. Verne only laughed. Worth a fortune, he said. He was all set for life, he said."

She picked up her fork, put it down again. "And then he scared Eve with it. Right after she got engaged to Thornton Grant she had to hand over some jewelry Frederick had given her. She was scared silly that Thornton would find out. And, acourse, Verne knew her father-in-law had paid her to stick by Cass during the trial. He got a lot of that, too. I never knew what he done with it. I never saw him unless he wanted something. Girls, I suppose, and nice clothes and a car. All like that. He had an apartment somewhere. Just every now and then he showed up."

She refused dessert. "Eve was almost out of her mind, I can tell you. Never knew when he'd come and want something. When she was asked to marry Mr. Thornton Grant, Verne intended to move right in. So Eve told him straight out that Thornton would drop her like a hot potato if he knew about her and Frederick, especially about the picture he'd painted, and there wouldn't be a cent for Verne.

"Well, Eve knew Miss Janet had got her share of the Grant money. Thornton told her. So she told him, just to get him off her back, give him someone else to work on. Though why she'd expect Miss Janet to pay Verne I don't know. So he took to keeping an eye on Miss Janet, to look over the prospect, like he said.

"Well, and then Verne kept on at Eve. Drove her wild. Called her up half the night so's she wouldn't be able to sleep. Upset things in her dressing room so's she could know she had to do something."

"Then your daughter knew all the time who was getting into her dressing room," O'Toole said. He had been staring at her in a kind of disbelief.

"Acourse. That's why she wanted Miss Grant to go to the theater. To hear him walk, to catch him. A kind of double-cross. Yeah, Eve was right smart in her way. But Verne wasn't anywheres around when Miss Grant got to the dressing room. He come in before the rehearsal started and mussed her up, bruised her arm, trying to make her give him some money. Then he went off somewheres. So it's too late now. And he was the only one who knew."

"Knew what?" O'Toole asked.

"Knew who killed Frederick."

O'Toole sat back, watching her. "Then you never believed Cass Grant killed him?"

She shook her head.

"What makes you so sure?"

"Because after Frederick died and Eve only had that three hundred thousand dollars, he went on getting money from somewhere. Who else? And neither Cass nor Janet had anything after their father died, so how could they of paid him? The worst of it is that Verne was the only one who really knew; he was the only one who knew who killed my girl." She looked up, her features raddled. "I guess, after all, I'd like that pecan pie a la mode."

FIFTEEN

The association between Mr. Potter and the lieutenant of detectives in the homicide department had been a long one. It had begun in mutual distrust and dislike when O'Toole had done his best to prove Mr. Potter to be a mass murderer and had, in the end, saved him from murder. It had grown, in mutual trust and liking, over a number of years. Now it seemed to be on the verge of dissolving into open enmity.

"But Cass Grant didn't kill Simmons!" Mr. Potter said heatedly. "You've got him nicely locked up and I don't know of a better alibi. There's no reason under heaven for continuing to hold him."

O'Toole lighted a cigarette, careful not to meet Mr. Potter's eyes.

"What evidence do you have?" Mr. Potter said insistently.

"Oh, save it." O'Toole was tired and irritable. "We're not holding Grant for the murder of Simmons. We haven't even charged him. You seem to forget we're interested in Eve Grant's killing. Her ex-husband had the strongest motive for her murder. Even if he didn't kill Frederick he knew damned well

217

that Eve had tried to railroad him to the chair. He hasn't the ghost of an alibi. He lied about spending the intermission in the theater lobby. Before we get done with him he is going to talk."

"Are you trying to tell me there are two killers? Who killed Simmons?"

O'Toole shook his head. "Damn it, I don't like this any better than you do, Potter. In fact, I hate it. I don't like sending women to the chair."

Mr. Potter's face was white. "What do you mean by that?"

"Just what you think I mean." O'Toole looked at his watch and stood up.

"Wait," Mr. Potter said. "You have no case against Miss Grant. She had every motive for keeping Simmons alive. He was her brother's only witness."

O'Toole looked at him in silence. Then he nodded. "Okay. Sit down, for God's sake, and stop prowling. I'll give it to you in a nutshell. Thornton tells Eve he has turned over Janet's money to her. Eve tells Simmons in order to take the heat off herself and give him another source of supply."

As Mr. Potter was silent, he went on. "Then Cass kills Eve. It's too much for him. Four years of brooding and now she's going to marry his cousin and get hold of his money as well. Simmons turns the heat on Janet. She can pay up or he won't help Cass. So Janet is scared. She arranges to meet Simmons, goes off in disguise, kills him while Cass has a nice unbreakable alibi, and saves the money at the same time."

"In that case," Mr. Potter said smoothly, a new note in his voice, "you've got to find a fourth person, haven't you?"

"What do you mean?"

"I mean the person who got that fourth print of the picture of Eve. The person whom Simmons had been blackmailing. It wasn't Janet Grant. She didn't have any money until three months ago." For the first time that morning he was cheerful and confident. "I want to get in to see Cass Grant."

"What are you up to?" O'Toole demanded with open suspicion.

Mr. Potter gave him a disarming smile. "I'm going to do your job for you," he said gently.

"This time," O'Toole said, "you're to keep out. For your own sake. And as of now."

Russlin's receptionist answered the telephone. Mr. Russlin was with a client. Was there a message? Yes, his secretary could talk.

"This is Mr. Russlin's secretary," said a cool voice.

"Hiram Potter. I want to see Cass Grant.

219

Can Mr. Russlin arrange it?"

The voice was not so cool now. She would inquire; she didn't know when Mr. Russlin would be free; he was a very busy man.

Mr. Potter set down the telephone. The young lady was not only unco-operative, she was frankly hostile. Russlin's office was on Madison Avenue in the 50's, a fairly small suite of rooms, with impersonal modernistic furniture in the reception room, and a forthcoming blonde at a table with a typewriter and a small switchboard. There seemed to be only three other rooms: Pete Russlin's office, a smaller one for his assistant, and a still smaller one for the secretary.

Mr. Russlin had been coming and going all day, the receptionist said, as though it gave her personal sorrow to disappoint Mr. Potter.

"Perhaps he left a message for me."

She plugged in, spoke and smiled brightly. "Mr. Russlin's secretary, Miss Clark, will see you. Through the gate and the first door on your left."

Miss Clark was young and pretty, with a trimly tailored suit and manner to match. But the eyes with their heavy overhanging lids, the sultry mouth were not tailored at all. She looked up from her desk.

"Mr. Potter? Mr. Russlin has arranged for you to see his client, Mr. Grant. All you have

220

to do is to give your name."

"Thank you." He pulled out the chair across from her and sat down. He opened his cigarette case and held it out.

There was a brief hesitation while she summed him up, the hostility he had detected over the telephone clear in her face. He gave her a disarming smile.

"Thank you," she said at last, took a cigarette and let him light it.

For a moment he smoked in silence. "Why don't you like Cass Grant?" he asked at length.

"Why should I?" Anger vibrated in her voice. "I've been working here for seven years. I watched Mr. Russlin build a fine legal practice. Then he got entangled with the Grants. He came as close as a man could to getting himself disbarred just in order to save that — that criminal murderer. And from that time on, though he works like a dog, his clients have been different. The shady ones. The grafters. The people trying to get away with something. He's never made it back again."

"One thing he succeeded at," Mr. Potter said quietly, "was in having a loyal secretary."

Some of the anger died out of her but her color rose. She was in love with her employer. Mr. Potter wondered whether the lawyer had ever suspected it.

"He works so hard," she said, "all that terrific energy but —" She made an angry gesture. "The money comes in but it's not what he really wants. He wants — he deserves — respect as a lawyer. He's truly brilliant. But his career — from his standpoint — is a failure."

Mr. Potter shook his head sympathetically.

"And do you suppose Janet Grant cares what she has done to him? Not she! Cold-blooded. Selfish. All she cares about is her nutty brother. Pete — Mr. Russlin did his best to make her see that she shouldn't get Cass out. But now, when he has killed again, what does he do? He takes on his defense."

She ground out her cigarette, took a long breath. "Well, you can see the guy if you want to, but if I were you, I'd be careful. He ought to be in a straitjacket."

"You're sure he's crazy, aren't you?"

"Have you heard the news today?" she asked.

"What news?"

"That head-shrinker Janet," she spat out the girl's name, "brought over here. Dr. Beldner."

"What about him?"

"He was killed early this morning in Switzerland by a patient he'd just ordered released."

"That's — bad news," Mr. Potter said,

when the silence had been prolonged beyond endurance.

Miss Clark smiled. "You never know," she said, "when these things are hereditary. Good afternoon." She turned back to the typewriter.

Something had happened to Cass Grant's face. The look of grim purpose that had stamped it during the television interview was gone. The facial muscles had slackened, the mouth was loose. The man wasn't even putting up a fight.

He nodded apathetically to Mr. Potter and stood leaning on the back of the chair across the table as though he were an old man.

"Who sent you here? Friend of Thornton's, aren't you? Will you please get the hell out. I don't want you or any of his friends." His expression changed. "And if you're a reporter —"

Mr. Potter revealed no trace of the profound shock he had experienced in seeing the change that a few hours had wrought in Cass.

"I am not a reporter. I am not particularly friendly with your cousin. And you may not want me but, by God, you need me."

Cass stared at him with a faint stirring of interest. "Do I indeed? What makes you so important to me?"

Mr. Potter smiled suddenly. "For one thing, I'm just about the only human being who is convinced that you didn't kill Maitland Frederick. And," he added clearly, "I suspect that I'm the only human being who is convinced you didn't kill Eve Grant. I think you are the victim of a very slick frame."

Cass's hands tightened on the back of the chair.

"And," Mr. Potter went on deliberately, "I'll prove it before I get done. If, that is, you stop acting like a zombie and put your wits to work to help me. For God's sake, man, sit down and relax. They won't let me spend the rest of the day with you. There's no time to waste."

Without taking his eyes off Mr. Potter's face, Cass pulled out the chair and sat down. "I don't get it. What's in this for you? If you've got the brains God gave a duck you'd know as well as I do that I'm for it again. Not even Pete Russlin could help me now. You can't ra'ar back and pass a miracle twice. Anyhow," he clutched the arms of his chair until his knuckles were white, "I'd as soon be dead as go back to Wentworth. Sooner. At least, with the electric chair the hell stops eventually."

Mr. Potter lighted a cigarette, a slight, relaxed-looking man, with an innocuously pleasant face. "Of course, if you aren't willing to put up a fight, you'll make it a lot tougher for yourself."

"Put up a fight! God! What with?"

"The truth," Mr. Potter said unexpectedly. "The whole truth. So far you've never told it, not even when your life was at stake. In fact, for my money, at the Frederick trial only one witness told the truth."

"Who was that?"

"Your sister." After a moment's pause, Mr. Potter added, "That's why I am here. I promised her I would help."

This time the two men exchanged a long look. Cass said rather painfully, "Russlin's in love with her. He always has been. I thought, way back there, she'd have married him if it hadn't been for me." He added rather awkwardly, "I just thought you ought to know the score before you — got involved."

You can learn a great deal about a person who takes honesty for granted, even if it means losing the only life-line in sight, Mr. Potter thought. He grinned. "I've been getting involved in sticky cases for over eight years."

"Oh. I sort of gathered — oh — well — what do we do now?"

"If you are willing to play ball, suppose you tell me every detail you can remember about the murder."

"But I don't know a thing!" Cass protested. "I'll swear on anything you like that I never went backstage."

"Not that murder. Maitland Frederick's."

"I don't get this," Cass admitted.

"For the love of God, start talking!" Mr. Potter said sharply. "Get going!"

"Where do I start?"

"At the beginning. With that morning."

Cass had been out with a prospect who had just come into money and was in the market for three cars: a sports model, a station wagon, a small car for his wife. One of those things that simply don't happen. So he had spent hours demonstrating cars.

"I sold him all three," he concluded, with an echo of that old astonishment, that old triumph in his voice. His eyes, too, Mr. Potter was relieved to see, had lost their apathy. They were alert and intelligent. "And the time checked out, nine in the morning until after three. The customer testified to that. We were together all the time."

Well, he'd felt pretty jubilant and he'd hurried home to tell Eve. They were going to celebrate, do it up brown. Dinner and a theater and a night club. Eve — for a moment Cass broke off and then added flatly that Eve had always loved the bright lights, and he hadn't had much money for things like that

226

after his marriage. Kept rather short.

As he went up the steps, he saw Thornton waiting at the door. The butler of the time, Cass couldn't remember his name, Gherkins or something like that, let them in.

Mr. Potter interrupted. "Was Thornton a frequent visitor?"

Once a month for dinner, maybe. They weren't particularly close. Thornton was older than his cousins and their interests were different. Actually, his father had liked Thornton far more than his children did. For one thing, they were both book collectors, though Thornton was a classical scholar and his father a lover of books, but without a specialty.

"So far as I recall," Mr. Potter said, frowning, "no check-up was even made of how Thornton had spent the day, how his time was accounted for."

"But look here," Cass protested, "Thornton couldn't have had anything to do with it."

"Couldn't he?"

"But why?" Cass asked blankly.

"Eve. He was planning to marry her at the time of her death. His interest in her might have started a long time ago."

"She was marrying him for his money," Cass said. "Stands to reason. And at the time Frederick died, Thornton didn't have my share of the money. Anyhow, he would hardly

227

have been likely to know about Eve's relationship with Frederick, to have a single reason for killing him."

"You know," Mr. Potter told him frankly, "It's a wonder to me that you escaped the chair. You seem to be doing your damnedest to clear everyone else and convict yourself."

"God forbid!" Cass said piously. For the first time he grinned. "I'm as ready as the next man to railroad someone else to the chair to save my own skin, only, damn it all, not Thornton. It isn't in him. The Grant temper skipped him. Jan and I got his share. God knows. Thornton's feelings have been in a deepfreeze all his life."

"Perhaps Eve helped to defrost them," Mr. Potter suggested mildly.

Cass shrugged. "She sure as hell had the equipment for it. And there's one thing good that has come out of this. Thornton had to turn over Jan's money. She thought it was just because she could put him in an embarrassing spot by telling the papers he wouldn't give her the money to fight for my release. Of course, it was because he intended to marry Eve and he didn't dare do that while he was known to hold out on Jan's part of the estate. That would be a bit too raw."

Deftly Mr. Potter prodded him back to the Frederick murder.

"Dad was in bed with a bout of flu and Thornton had come to see him. He went into the library, I think, while Gherkins or Wilkins or whoever the hell it was went up to Dad's room."

Mr. Potter interrupted again. "How do you know that?"

"Jan found him there just a few minutes later. No time to go anywhere else."

"Go on."

"Jan cornered me and told me about Mrs. Frederick's telephone call. I thought the damned woman was lying and I started over to tell her so. Or that Frederick, without a model, on his own —"

Cass accepted a cigarette from Mr. Potter. It wobbled between his lips while Mr. Potter lighted it. Cass took a deep steadying breath. "Well, Jan said Eve knew about it and I'd better talk to her first. Eve — denied it, of course. She cried and clung to me and said why didn't I wait a while to cool and then she started —" Dull color swept over the face that had been bloodless. "Well, hell, it was her best weapon, of course; that and her beauty."

"Delaying tactics."

"What do you mean?"

"She called someone as soon as Janet had told her about Mrs. Frederick."

Cass stared at him. Then, looking sick, he crushed out the unsmoked cigarette. He had gone over to see Frederick himself. No need to bring Mrs. Frederick into it, after all. A maid let him in; he found Mrs. Frederick and Thornton talking in the drawing room. They had tried to stop him. He'd gone straight past them and out to the studio.

"I've told all this over and over," he said impatiently.

"Not all of it," Mr. Potter reminded him. "This time I want it all."

Cass had flung open the studio door, gone inside. Frederick was lying on the floor, dead. He had been strangled. And on an easel was the painting of Eve.

"I burned it in the fireplace. It was quite a job."

"Why did you deny the existence of the painting at the trial?"

"Because it gave me such a lovely motive," Cass said bluntly. "But, God, she wasn't worth killing him for. I didn't kill Frederick, Potter. Eve just was not worth it. Nothing seemed to be worth anything."

The two men were silent, each sunk in his own thoughts. Then Mr. Potter said, "Frederick didn't strangle himself. It seems completely impossible for his wife to have done so. If I were to accept Thornton's word that he heard someone moving around in the studio, and your word that Frederick was dead when you went in, then whom did Thornton hear and how did that third person get in there unseen? He had only two or three minutes, at most."

"That's funny," Cass said. "All I've been thinking about is who. I never wondered how." He was interested now, ready to tackle the problem. "Well — are you familiar with the layout of the two houses?"

"Only in a general way. I haven't been through them."

"They take up all the frontage on the street. Each one has an areaway with an entrance to the basement. Each one has French doors leading from the small morning room at the back on the first floor into the garden."

"Then why didn't you go straight out to the studio through your own house instead of through the Frederick house?"

"Because we'd been rebuilding a brick terrace in back and one of the workmen accidentally broke some panes in one of the French doors. It was boarded up for that one day."

"Then a third person, and there has to be a third person, could enter either house by the front door or the door to the basement through the areaway, but he could reach the studio only through the morning room of the Frederick house on the day of the murder."

"It's worse than that. Both front doors were kept locked. That was brought out at the trial. There were servants in the basements of both houses at the time of the murder. Unless your third person was invisible — don't you see, it's impossible."

Mr. Potter sighed. "You — Thornton — an outsider. He got in somehow. Now think!"

Cass grunted. "Jan tried to prove there was someone at the studio with her tall story about the limping window cleaner. That window cleaner was invented, Potter! It was Jan's idea, her girl-scout deed for the day."

"And that," Mr. Potter said, "brings us up to this morning. Janet — your sister — got a telephone call from a man who identified himself as her limping man. He wanted fifty thousand dollars to tell her who killed Frederick and Eve."

Cass stared at him. "Good God! And she fell for that? The poor kid."

"She kept the appointment but she didn't hand over the money."

"Thank heaven for small blessings. I hope they got him."

"Someone did. He was strangled."

"Dead?"

"Very. His wife identified the body as that

of Verne Simmons, Eve's stepfather. He was far gone with tuberculosis of the bones. He's the limping man, all right, the man who had been pestering Eve."

Cass half rose from his chair. "Potter, what about Jan?"

"I sent her home. She's all right, Grant. The money is all right."

"The hell with the money! The police are going to believe that Jan was trying to cover for me. What are they going to do to her?"

"Stop shouting and sit down." Mr. Potter waited until Cass sat back in his chair, his hand opening and closing on the arm. "Janet is in no immediate danger of arrest. For one thing, she couldn't have killed Frederick. For another, a close check on her bank account is bound to reveal that she hasn't been Simmons' blackmail victim. The police are going to start all over again and before they get through they'll find the man who killed Frederick, the man who killed your wife, the man who killed Simmons."

"You seem pretty sure of yourself," Cass said curiously.

"I have to be. There must be no more mistakes, no more miscarriages of justice."

"Get hold of Russlin right away, will you, Potter? He loves Jan. He'll think of something, find some way." His mouth twisted wryly. "He's the hell of a good friend. He really pulled one out of the hat to keep me from the chair and then he managed to get me transferred from the state asylum and into Wentworth. It damaged his reputation, you know. People thought he'd pulled a fast one. He got a lot of criticism; he's never really recovered from it professionally. The kind of clients he'd like to have shy clear of that sort of thing. He — we owe him more than we can ever repay."

He accepted another cigarette and this time he smoked it. "All I'm trying to say is that Pete Russlin is a damned good guy." Cass looked soberly at Mr. Potter. "There aren't too many people whom you can trust all the way."

Mr. Potter smiled. "Jack shall have Jill and all will be well."

"I didn't mean —"

"I'm not in the running," Mr. Potter told him quietly. "That you may be quite sure of. But Russlin and I can at least put our heads together and try a little teamwork."

He got up quickly, taking Cass by surprise. "Oh, by the way, there are a couple of questions. Have you ever read *The Metamorphoses*?"

Cass looked his astonishment. "Yes, picked it up at Wentworth. Matter of fact, I read straight through the library there and I was starting a second round when Jan's Swiss wonder got me out."

"What did you think of it?"

"Just a lot of changes run on the same theme. The classics aren't especially my meat, but the book made an impression, made me look like a highbrow."

Mr. Potter shook hands, started toward the door, turned back abruptly. "Where did you spend that twenty-minute intermission last night?"

"At a bar on Seventh Avenue. Seeing Eve on top of the world, everything rosy for her, and me loused up for life — okay, self-pity, if you like — but I felt like tying one on. Actually, I had only one drink. I decided I wouldn't give that little witch the satisfaction of seeing me come apart at the seams."

"Which bar?"

"Tim's, I think it's called. The first one I came to. Big and dark and crowded. A jukebox. I got a feeling maybe a little betting on the horses was going on."

"Anyone notice you?"

"I wouldn't know." Cass's face was bitter again. "Probably. The playboy killer. A lot of people know my pan by now, wouldn't you think?"

"At least," Mr. Potter said, "we'll hope so."

SIXTEEN

"Stop here," Janet called and the taxi drew in at the curb. Half a block away she could see the crowd outside the twin houses, the press cars, the photographers, the idly curious, the patrolling policeman.

There was no help for it. She'd have to go through the crowd to reach the house and this time without the disguise which she had left in the suitcase at Grand Central Station. That disguise, that furtive escape from the house — she realized with a sinking heart how suspicious they would appear.

She walked swiftly toward her house, head high, looking straight ahead. A flashbulb exploded; a photographer backing away from her, snapped a picture, an onlooker with a movie camera was recording her approach to the house.

"Miss Grant, how do you feel about your sister-in-law's murder? . . . Is your brother going to have Russlin as his lawyer again? . . . Why did you go to the theater last night?"

She shook her head but she was surrounded, she could not get near the door. From bitter experience she knew that any comment, however harmless it appeared, would be blown up and distorted until it became unrecognizable.

An officer climbed out of a radio car. "Get moving."

"Look this way, Miss Grant . . . Thanks a lot . . . Will you make a statement about your brother's arrest?"

"But he wasn't —" She stopped short.

The officer took her arm. "Get lost," he advised the crowd, and steered her toward the door. She rang the bell and then remembered that the house was empty, the servants had all gone. She fumbled for a key. There was another flash and she realized with a cringing feeling that the picture had been taken with the policeman holding her arm, as though she were in his custody.

"Thank you," she said as she went inside. "And, please, officer, can't you make them go away?"

He gave her an odd look. "I thought you were still in the house. How did you get out?"

"Through the areaway," she admitted.

"Take my advice, sister. Stay put."

She nodded and the door closed behind her. It seemed to her that weeks had passed since she had escaped from the house, collected the money and gone to meet the limping man. In her own room she slipped into a dressing gown and slippers and stretched on the gold

237

chaise longue. She had to sort out her thoughts, to get things clear. Instead, she fell almost instantly into a deep sleep.

A bell was ringing somewhere. Half awake, she reached for the telephone that she had gilded to match the draperies. Her hand dropped. There was a persistent hammering. She opened her eyes and noticed her dressing gown. She blinked in surprise. What in the world was she doing? She looked at her watch. Four o'clock. She had been asleep for three hours. That hammering — what on earth were the servants doing? Someone was working on the knocker with a tremendous clatter.

She remembered then that she was alone in the house, that the staff had left. She ran downstairs and peered cautiously outside. A patient crowd still waited for something to happen. Pete Russlin, not patient at all, was at the door. He began a fresh assault on the knocker.

She slid back the bolt and let him in. He closed and locked the door and took her tightly in his arms. "Thank God! I was afraid something had happened to you. Another moment and I'd have broken the door in."

"You nearly did. Oh, Pete, I'm so glad to see you!" She released herself and saw for the first time how haggard he looked.

"I came as soon as I got your message. Rotten luck that I had to be in court when you called." He looked around. "What's wrong with that staff of yours? I made enough noise to wake the dead."

She told him as she preceded him into the library.

"Then you're all alone here? But that's impossible. Let me call a hotel and make a reservation for you."

She shook her head.

"But you can't stay here alone."

"Better than a hotel with people staring as I go in and out. At least there's privacy here, and I gave up the apartment."

"But this isn't safe. Remember what your caretaker Marker said about someone getting in? Please, darling, do as I ask. I'll worry if you stay in this damned house."

"It's no use, Pete, I'm going to stay."

Something in her voice made him give up with a helpless gesture. "At least, get someone to stay with you."

"I'll have the police chaperoning me until this thing is cleared up," she said dryly.

His expression changed. "Janet! Why don't you marry me right away? We can do it in three days. Then I'll have the right to stay here and look after you. Let's do it, darling."

Janet tried to speak lightly though her throat was choked at the thought of this ultimate sacrifice of his career. "What knight-errantry."

"I've waited a long time." There was no answering lightness in his tone. "A very long time. There's nothing trivial about this thing to me, my darling. I knew, as long as Cass was at Wentworth, there was no hope, but now — I love you very much, Janet. This is the best way, the right way for us both. After all, we've loved each other for a long time. It's only a way of telling the world that we do. Don't make me wait any longer. Let me take care of you."

"Oh, Pete. I'm sorry. So very sorry." Her hands held him off.

He lifted her chin, looked deeply into her eyes. "It would be all right, Janet. It would be good, good and rich. I'd make you happy. Don't force me to wait again until Cass is out of this."

"But I'm not, Pete. It's not because of Cass. It — I'm desperately sorry but I can't, Pete."

He turned away, walked the length of the room, stood staring blindly at the tapestry on the wall. "There's someone else, isn't there?" The voice was drained of feeling, so flat that it didn't sound like Pete's vibrant voice at all. "You've changed. You're in love with some-one else."

Janet did not answer. She sat quietly, waiting for him to come back to her. It was a long time before he turned around to meet her anxious eyes and, after all, he was the same Pete with the same affectionate smile.

"Now then," he began, pulling up a chair to face her, "let's forget Russlin the lover and come back to Russlin the lawyer. Let's talk about Cass and start mapping our strategy."

"There's something else, Pete, I've got to tell you first. Something terrible has happened."

She described the telephone call from the man who had claimed to be her limping man, his claim that he could clear Cass, his demand for fifty thousand dollars. She told the story quietly, ending with the man's murder almost before her eyes and her meeting with Mr. Potter.

He listened to her, white-faced, his eyes never leaving her own. He gripped her hands until he hurt her. At length, when she was silent, he expelled a long breath.

"My God! What a frightful risk you ran! Suppose this fellow had heard you, suppose he'd had to get rid of you! God, Janet!" He pulled out his handkerchief and wiped away the drops of perspiration on his forehead, mopped his face.

"He did hear me. I called out from downstairs. That's," Janet licked dry lips, "when

241

he killed the limping man. I could hear the poor fellow's heels drumming on the floor and then the other man ran, opened a window, climbed down the fire escape."

"Did you get a look at him?"

"I didn't even try, Pete. I saw the dead man and I nearly fainted. By that time it would have been too late, anyhow. He'd had plenty of time to get away."

"So then you called Potter," Pete said slowly, and she was aware of the stirring of jealousy, of pain in his face.

"You were in court," she reminded him. "Your office had said so. I did call you first. And I — the police haven't given the Grants much of a break, have they? So there was no one else."

"But why Potter?"

"Because he was the only person who ever believed that the limping man existed. The police didn't. You didn't. Even Cass. You all thought I was lying to protect him. And now the man is dead and there is no one left to clear Cass. No one at all."

"Right now," Pete said grimly, "I'm not concerned about Cass. He's out of this. But you are behind the eight ball. You're the one who has to be cleared."

"Yes, I know. The police won't believe me, about the dead man having evidence to clear

Cass, I mean. They'll think he was blackmailing me and I killed him for that."

"Hey," Pete said, "we're going to fight it out on this line if it takes all summer." He went out into the hall where he had left his overcoat on a chair, came back to toss a package into her lap.

"Gadget I picked up. Now that you're alone here it may come in handy."

She opened it and started back. "Not a revolver! I'd be terrified even to have it around."

"It's a flashlight made to look like a revolver. Better keep it handy, just in case."

She laughed and put it on the library table. "You are incorrigible."

"At least, I've made you laugh. Now, Janet, tell me just what happened when you went backstage with Eve last night."

He listened, asked a question now and then, made notes. "And you didn't actually see the limping man's face. Just heard him?"

"I didn't see anyone but Eve and Mrs. Simmons and a couple of stagehands. The members of the cast were in their dressing rooms changing for the second act. All I saw of the limping man was a dim figure in the alley."

"Did Cass tell you where he really spent that intermission?" Pete asked. "You realize,

243

don't you, that he couldn't have stayed in the lobby or Sanders Newton would have seen him. And Thornton absolutely denied he had stayed there."

"We didn't have any chance to talk to each other last night. The policeman who was watching us just sat there, saying, 'No talking, please. The lieutenant will see you soon.' "

"Look here, darling, there's one thing we've got to face. Cass could have gone up that fire escape and hidden in the storeroom while you were with Eve. He could have killed her after you ran down the fire escape. We've got to have a damned good alibi for him this time. Airtight."

"I know." She met his eyes levelly. "Don't be so unhappy about it, Pete. I see as clearly as you do that, the way things stand, it's going to rest between Cass and me. One of us — or both. The only chance we have is to find the real murderer."

"I wish to God," he said violently, "you hadn't gone backstage with Eve. I'm guilty as hell. You know that, don't you?"

"Guilty?"

"I advised you and Cass to go to that damned rehearsal. But I thought it might ease tensions, keep things smooth when Eve married Thornton."

"There's no point in blaming yourself, Pete. The thing is done now. We went to the theater of our own free will. At least, no one forced us to go, not even Eve."

"Yes," he said heavily, "it's done." He got up. "I'm going down to see Cass and make him tell me where he was during that intermission. We'll have to dig up some witnesses. Damn it all, someone must have recognized him. His pictures have been plastered all over the place." He crushed Janet's hands in his. "Keep your chin up, kid."

The telephone rang and she picked it up.

"Miss Grant? . . . Hiram Potter. Will you do something for me, please?"

"If I possibly can. Mr. Potter, did —"

"Later. I'd like you to go to that window in your room where you stood and watched the window cleaner come toward your house. Will you do that in, say, fifteen minutes?"

"Of course," Janet said in astonishment. She put down the telephone, repeated Mr. Potter's request to Pete, and at the end of a quarter of an hour, which stretched interminably, they went up to her bedroom, looked out on the snow-covered garden and hedges, on the studio at the back.

"How did Potter get into this thing in the

245

first place?" Pete asked.

"He is Graham Collinge's house guest and he just went along to the dress rehearsal for fun."

"Chance?" Pete shook his head. "Somehow, I doubt that. Potter's an odd sort of duck. He gets involved in things. He's a very tough proposition, though you might not think so to look at him."

"I'm not so sure," Janet said slowly.

"I used to know his lawyer. We were in the same class at law school."

"Then you've met him before through this mutual friend."

"No," Pete said, "Potter saw to it that our mutual friend went to the electric chair." His hand suddenly clamped down on her shoulder. Janet lifted her head, listening, lips parted as though helping her straining ear to hear. Overhead someone was walking. For a moment the two stood motionless.

"There's someone up there," Janet whispered unnecessarily.

Pete turned toward the door. Someone ran down the stairs, stood in the doorway.

"I didn't mean to startle you," Mr. Potter said, seeing Janet's wide frightened eyes. "But there wasn't any other way to prove it."

"Prove what?" Pete demanded.

"Prove that Miss Grant couldn't have seen

246

the limping man come through the garden four years ago."

"But I did," Janet cried. — "I did! I thought you believed me."

"Did you see me coming through the garden a few minutes ago?"

She shook her head, dazed.

Pete spoke suddenly, his comforting hand still on her shoulder, sustaining her. "As your lawyer, Janet, I suggest that you don't answer any more questions. Leave this to me."

Mr. Potter caught Janet's eyes, held them. "The man who was strangled at the warehouse today has been identified. He was Eve's stepfather, Verne Simmons. He was your limping man, Miss Grant. He had tuberculosis of the bones. Now he wasn't a tall man, just my height, in fact, and the hedges are six feet high. It wasn't Simmons you saw. Someone else was wearing that white painter's cap."

She shook her head. "You must be mistaken. I saw the man on the ladder, looking through the skylight. I saw his clumsy lurch when he climbed down. I saw the white cap in the garden, and I heard that halting step upstairs. Then Eve cried out when he struck her."

"Oh, Simmons was here," Mr. Potter agreed. "And when I think of the chances they took, it staggers me. A ten-to-one shot of getting away with it without being seen by someone."

"They?"

"Oh, yes. When Simmons came here he brought the murderer with him. He's the one who was wearing the white cap, you know."

"And how the hell did you get in this house?" Pete demanded.

SEVENTEEN

How had the murderer gotten into the house? How had he even gotten to the studio unseen? Not who or why — but how?

From the moment Mr. Potter left Cass he began to grapple with the puzzle. Unless the killer had been Mrs. Frederick, Cass, or Thornton, a new approach had to be made to the whole problem. For the time being, Mr. Potter pushed aside the thought of Thornton. Not that he believed the man could be eliminated entirely but because, whether he was guilty or not, the presence of Simmons at the studio remained unexplained, as well as his later appearance in the third-floor suite where Eve had lived.

The front doors of both houses were locked. The areaway doors were equally improbable because there had been servants in the basements of both houses. That left an approach from 67th Street to the studio, but it still did not account for Simmons' getting inside the Grant house unseen. The only entrance from the garden was the door of the morning room in each house, and that day the garden door of the Grant house had been boarded up. Leaving what?

Twin houses. *Twin* houses! Mr. Potter had been walking almost blindly along the street. Now he looked for a public telephone, found one in a cigar store. Mrs. Frederick answered at once.

"Yes, when they were first built the houses opened into each other . . . the drawing room and a door on the third floor. . . . I don't think it would be possible. The drawing room door was plastered over and it has been a solid wall ever since we lived there. The door on the third floor was sealed on both sides. . . . No, I turned over all my keys to Thornton Grant when his uncle gave him control of the property and I moved out. . . . I'll call him at once. . . . Well, Janet had a set of keys, of course. Probably Eve did. . . . Yes, it was ridiculous, but the keys fitted both houses. Janet's grandmother didn't believe in separate residences or in privacy for her son, and we just never bothered to change them. . . . So far as I know, there are no other keys in existence. I," she hesitated, "I hope you are going to be able to help them, Janet and Cass."

"I hope so, too. Thank you, Mrs. Frederick."

A frigid Thornton handed Mr. Potter the keys to the Frederick house. "Though what you expect to find there after nearly four years, I can't imagine. Mrs. Frederick cleared

250

out the house. It's empty."

"I don't know either," Mr. Potter told him cheerfully.

He stopped at a drugstore to make a purchase, thinking about the conversation Eve Grant's maid had overheard: "You're in this, too, darling." You're in this, too. You're in this, too.

He leaned against the wall of the telephone booth in the drugstore, fighting the idea that had come into his mind. It wasn't possible. He closed the door and dialed O'Toole. He talked fast.

"Well," O'Toole said at length, trying to keep the satisfaction out of his voice, "it sounds like the girl, after all. That's what I —"

"We've got to clear as we go, of course," Mr. Potter said flatly. "I'm doing what I can from this end, but there are some points." He listed them while O'Toole made notes.

"Okay," O'Toole said. "Have I got this straight? Look for a discarded raincoat, probably in the theater; check the stage set for fluoroscin; find out how long Janet Grant has been shacking up with Pete Russlin. How did you get on to that?"

"His secretary is in love with him and jealous as hell of Janet. I think she knew she had competition."

"Uh-huh. Call — who's that? Kenneth Morton at the City Bank? Use your name . . . Old lady in tenement across from the warehouse. Check Tim's Bar on Seventh Avenue not far from the theater. . . . All other bars in the immediate vicinity. The what — Oh, I see. Then you think they were in it together."

Mr. Potter made no comment. His face was grim, older.

O'Toole added, "How about the killing of Dr. Beldner? This patient he thought was cured? Sometimes it runs in the family, doesn't it? . . . Yep, *The Metamorphoses*. But we — okay, but it will be the hell of a job. . . . The garden? That was four years ago, man. How —"

"You'll find a way," Mr. Potter said. "You'll have to."

After he had telephoned Janet Grant, Mr. Potter hailed a cab and asked to be dropped at the corner of Fifth Avenue and 67th Street. He walked slowly along the block. Halfway down the street an ornamental iron gate on the sidewalk shut off a narrow stretch of lawn with flower beds, one of those unexpected oases that make New York endlessly fascinating.

Mr. Potter did not hesitate or look around.

With an assured air he reached over the gate to release the catch and walked in, shutting it behind him. Then he glanced up. The buildings on both side had heavily curtained windows to insure privacy. He went through to the back where there were some stunted trees in tubs and, apparently in the summer, iron tables and striped umbrellas to give the illusion of a real garden. Or perhaps it was used as a garden. New Yorkers, as dance floors in night clubs evidence, are adept at accommodating themselves to confined spaces.

At the back, dividing it from the 68th Street property, there was a low hedge. Mr. Potter turned for a swift look up at the curtained windows but he could see no one. Again he wondered at the desperate chance that had been taken by anyone who had come this way. He stepped over the hedge and around the side of the studio. For a moment he looked at the tall hedges, then he turned toward the Frederick house.

The third key unlocked the French doors and he went inside. On the day of the murder Mrs. Frederick had talked to Thornton in the drawing room at the front of the house. The thing could have been done, with the devil's own luck.

The house was cold and empty. The furniture had long since been removed. Outside the morning room a narrow stairway had apparently been used by the servants.

Mr. Potter went up the stairs to the third floor and looked at the door that had once opened into the other house. There was no seal on it now. He tried the keys Thornton had given him. None of them worked. Then he pulled out the pair of eyebrow tweezers which he had bought in the drugstore, and knelt on the floor, maneuvering them delicately. They caught, turned. He opened the door and found himself in the hallway of the Grant house. He ran down the stairs.

Janet and Pete had been standing close together, his hand protectively on her shoulder, like allies facing an enemy.

"So that's it," he concluded. "That's how they got in. I suspect Eve let them out the front door as soon as the coast was clear."

"From the beginning," Janet said, "I've been sure that she knew who killed Mr. Frederick but she let that horror happen to Cass! How could she?"

"I suspect," Mr. Potter told her, "that Eve was scared out of her wits, and its my impression that she had a very strong sense of self-preservation."

"She had," Pete said dryly. "The hell of it was that she looked so young and innocent and beautiful, and Cass swore there was no painting; so I couldn't hammer at her in court. The jury would have thought she was being bullied. I was hamstrung."

"At least," Janet said, "we know how someone has been getting into this house. I've thought all the time it was Eve because she had keys."

"Getting in?" Mr. Potter repeated sharply.

She told him Marker's story about someone searching the house and about Eve's telephone call on the day of the murder.

Mr. Potter grinned at Pete. "That gives you one nice point for the defense. Thank God, your watchman reported to the police."

"I'll play it for all it's worth," Pete assured him. "Any more tricks up your sleeve, man? I could use them. For God's sake, give!"

Mr. Potter nodded. "I told Cass that you and I would put in some useful teamwork."

"You've seen Cass?" Janet exclaimed eagerly.

"This afternoon. He's all set to put up the fight of his life."

"For his life," she reminded him somberly.

"Now, darling," Pete said, "you mustn't lose hope. We haven't even begun to fight."

"Eve's maid supports your story about something Eve had lost. She heard her on the telephone, not long ago, saying frantically, 'You've got to try again. After all, darling, you're in this, too.' "

"If she was talking to Thornton," Pete said viciously, "I'll rip his hide off in court. I'll strip him of all his pretensions. I'll make him sweat the way Cass has sweated. And will I love it!"

"That would be a pleasure to watch," Mr. Potter agreed warmly. "But meantime — there's Janet."

"What about Janet?" Automatically Pete's arm reached out to hold her, protect her.

"The murder of Simmons. For the life of me, I don't understand why O'Toole has waited this long."

And downstairs the doorbell rang.

After all, O'Toole had not come to make an arrest, though there was a moment when, seeing his grim face, Pete expected him to pull out a warrant. He had come in person, he said, to tell Janet the good news. Cass was to be released later in the evening.

After his stunned surprise, Pete's narrow face lighted up. "Thank God!"

O'Toole made no comment. Pete gave him a worried look. When you come to a house to bring good news in person you don't, as a role, carry with you the aura of an executioner.

"You'll get him and see he comes right

home, won't you?" Janet urged him.

Pete smiled down at her, kissed her lightly on the lips. "Everything is under control."

When Pete had gone, O'Toole reached for his hat. "Your brother should be home soon."

"I'm so glad."

"Coming, Potter?"

With a long look at the girl, Mr. Potter accompanied O'Toole. "Have you anyone watching her?"

O'Toole grinned. "What do you think?"

An official car was waiting and he gave an address in the Bronx. The sky had cleared but the early evening was already almost dark and it was bitterly cold.

At length, Mr. Potter, stirring uneasily as O'Toole remained silent, told him about his discovery of the way someone had got into the Grant house.

"That's helpful." Unexpectedly O'Toole grinned. "Of course, you ought to be charged with breaking and entering. How did you learn to pick a lock?"

"Just natural sin. Are you going to talk?" Mr. Potter's voice was strained. "Why are you letting Cass Grant go?"

"We've been busy since you called. We checked on Tim's Bar. Cass Grant was there practically the whole twenty minutes, just staring at his glass. He had only one drink and didn't finish that. There were three or four people, aside from the bartenders, who recognized him, and they — the bartenders, at least — were very forthcoming. Looks as though they are taking bets on the ponies as a sideline. They don't want any trouble with us."

"So Cass has an alibi for Eve's murder." When O'Toole made no further comment, Mr. Potter implored him, "Open up, will you?" and the detective began to laugh.

"Okay. Haskel called in. There was a discarded raincoat backstage. No identification but there was fluoroscin on the back. And he found what you were looking for on a table on the stage set and also in the storeroom."

"And you're just — letting him go free?"

"I sent a guy down to talk to the people in the tenement across from the warehouse. He'll call in as soon as he gets anything. Got another one checking on Russlin's apartment. He took along a newspaper picture of Janet. I called your banker friend myself. It's beginning to add up."

"Where are we going now?"

"We've found Simmons' apartment in the Bronx."

The manager in charge of the big housing development looked at O'Toole's credentials without pleasure. Sure he had a pass key.

What had Simmons been up to? He got himself killed, the lieutenant explained.

"Lame like he was, I always thought he'd get caught someday crossing the street. Had to go so slow." The manager was interested but not particularly distressed.

"Did you know him well?"

The manager shrugged. "Saw him once a month when he paid his rent, always in cash."

"Didn't that surprise you?"

The manager gave him a sardonic look. "Brother, in this business nothing surprises you. At least he paid. We try to size up people because we don't go asking for trouble and we don't want the noisy ones if we can prevent it. Simmons was no trouble; he paid regular and he was quiet."

O'Toole waited and the manager fidgeted. "He was quite a one for the girls, but no noisy parties."

Simmons had lived there for four years. He had a five-room apartment in Unit Ten. The manager led the way. Unit Ten looked exactly like the other fifteen buildings. Simmons had an apartment on the fourth floor front. The manager unlocked the door and stood back to let Mr. Potter, O'Toole and the sergeant precede him. Then he looked around and whistled. "I didn't know he had so much dough."

The apartment was expensively furnished, with deep rugs, fine draperies and furniture that looked as though it had come from an excellent shop. There was a well-stocked bar and a wardrobe that consisted of a dozen tailormade suits, fine shirts and handmade shoes.

"Did he own a raincoat?" Mr. Potter asked.

The manager shook his head. "I don't think so. He was one of the diehards who still carry an umbrella."

O'Toole nodded. "That's all and thank you. We'll return the key when we have finished here." The manager took his departure rather reluctantly.

Methodically O'Toole and the sergeant began to search. By the end of a half hour O'Toole shook his head. "I feel as if we were on a treasure hunt."

From under the living room carpet they had retrieved five hundred dollars in one-hundred-dollar bills. The same amount was fastened to the bottom of a chair. A record album contained another five hundred dollars. There was a similar cache in a shoe and one inside the lining of a hat.

"At least," Mr. Potter said, looking at the growing pile of money, "there will be a nice nest egg for his widow."

"Blackmail money," O'Toole pointed out.

"Who can claim it without asking for a free seat in the electric chair? What proof is there? Frederick is dead. Eve is dead."

Behind a loose tile in the shower there was a rubberized case for holding washcloths. O'Toole brought it out to add to the money he and the sergeant had been stacking on the end table beside Mr. Potter's chair. He opened the package, pulled out a small snapshot, held it to the light, and handed it to Mr. Potter.

Mr. Potter looked at it, handed it back as though eager to get rid of it. "So now we know what Simmons used for blackmail, what Eve had to pay him for."

"But he was getting regular money somewhere else," O'Toole reminded him. "After all, he saw a murder done."

"So you believe that at last."

O'Toole nodded. "You did a brilliant job of guessing there." He was not trying to make amends, just trying to be kind. "As a rule, no man can think straight when he's in love."

"And now?"

"Now we do some elimination so no slick lawyer can find a hole in this case."

"You have a case?"

"I will have and this time, Potter, it's going to stick."

"You're allowing a lot of freedom of action, aren't you?"

O'Toole grinned. "Not as much as you'd think."

O'Toole gave the driver Thornton's address and Mr. Potter said hastily, "Here is where I had better bow out. He doesn't like me at all."

"He's not going to like me either," O'Toole said.

The houseman admitted them at once and went upstairs. There were voices and then Thornton came down, followed by a portly man whom Mr. Potter recognized as Willis Kent, an attorney of considerable, and sound, reputation.

"My lawyer, Mr. Kent. Mr. Potter. Lieutenant O'Toole." Thornton looked at the sergeant, ignored him, turned to Mr. Potter. "Still scavenging?"

"Mr. Grant," his lawyer intervened, "perhaps you had better let me —" He did a double-take. "Hiram Potter? I know your aunt."

"You have my sympathy."

Kent chuckled jovially. "I see your point, but a well-meaning woman. Very well-meaning. I've followed your somewhat hectic career for some time." His eyes twinkled. "It will be a privilege to see you in action."

Thornton smiled thinly but Kent had developed a professional chuckle, a jolly sound that shook his plump body. He chuckled now. He was hell-bent, Mr. Potter decided, on being agreeable. The lawyer gave a quick look at his client who did not seem to be cooperating. Thornton sat stiffly in his chair, trying to hold his head still but, in spite of his efforts, it jerked to the right in that new habit it had acquired since the discovery of Eve's murder.

"How long is it going to take you to solve this thing?"

"Now, Mr. Grant," the lawyer put in placatingly, "I must warn you against making ill-advised statements."

"We haven't been playing around," O'Toole said calmly. "I've been kept busy. There was another murder around noon today." He paused for a moment. "Eve Grant's stepfather, Verne Simmons, was strangled. The doctor says he must have had quite a limp." There was a momentary silence. "Cass Grant has been released. He couldn't have killed Simmons."

"And Eve?"

"We've checked his alibi. Your cousin didn't kill her either, Mr. Grant. Every moment of his time during the intermission has been accounted for."

"I don't believe it." Thornton's head jerked.

263

Kent intervened. "What connection is there between Mrs. Grant's murder and that of her stepfather?"

"Simmons has been living on blackmail. He didn't get it from Cass or Janet Grant because they had no money. Not, that is, until Eve told him recently that Janet had been given her own money. I take it she learned that from you, Mr. Grant. This morning Simmons telephoned, demanding fifty thousand dollars to tell Janet who had killed Maitland Frederick and Eve."

"So it was Janet," Thornton said. "Well, it had to be one or the other of them."

"Mr. Grant!" Kent expostulated. "I must insist that you let me be your spokesman."

Thornton's head jerked, red flecks appeared in his eyes. "Can't you see the truth when it is before your eyes? She did this to give Cass an out. She hated Eve."

"Simmons lived on blackmail for years because he witnessed the killing of Maitland Frederick. I repeat, the Grants did not have the kind of money he demanded."

Thornton's head jerked. Jerked again.

"Are you trying to implicate Eve? Of all the damnable things to do! What is it, that old filthy story about a picture Frederick had painted of her?"

O'Toole reached in his pocket, pulled out

the rubberized case. He handed the snapshot to Thornton. "We found this hidden in Simmons' apartment."

Thornton stared at it, handed it to Kent.

"And now," O'Toole said briskly, "about your alibi for the intermission last night. You claimed to be in the lobby smoking."

"I'd forgotten to send Eve any flowers that day," Thornton said dully. "There was a shop down the street that keeps open at night. I went there, picked out some orchids because they were her favorite flowers. They were to be delivered at the theater at eleven, when I thought the rehearsal would be over."

The sergeant nodded. "They came."

"This was easy to check. Why did you hold out on me?" O'Toole asked.

Thornton's head jerked.

"Cass said he'd been in the lobby," Mr. Potter commented. "Thornton liked making it tough for his cousins when he could."

Thornton shouted, shocking them all. "Why did Cass stop with Frederick? Why didn't he kill them both? Why didn't he kill Eve?"

"Mr. Grant!" Kent's roar drowned out Thornton's loud voice. "Mr. Grant! You must not say another word. Is that clear?"

EIGHTEEN

Janet looked at her watch. Nearly seven. Cass would be home any minute. Nearly seven! No wonder she had a hollow feeling. She had eaten nothing all day except for a piece of toast.

Down in the kitchen she scrambled an egg and poured a glass of milk. When Cass came they would have cocktails and go out to dinner, some small place where they wouldn't be recognized. She was familiar with a number of obscure restaurants now. For four years she had eaten in them, sitting in corners, wearing dark glasses. Well, that was over now.

She kept repeating the phrase to herself but, somehow, it was meaningless. Even when she had finished the egg and drunk the milk, the hollow feeling remained, a feeling like fear. And that was nonsense. After all, Cass was free and nothing more could happen. Not possibly.

The doorbell rang, three short rings. Cass's old signal. She ran to open it. He stood smiling at her and she flung her arms around him.

"Oh, Cass. Cass!"

He grinned. The haggard look was gone, he was confident again. For the first time since Eve's murder the old carefree expression was

266

back on his face. "Hi, kid!"

"Was it all right?"

"Pete barged in, signed some papers, and out I walked. Not supposed to leave town, of course. I wanted to bring him home to celebrate, but he said he'd call later. I told him we'd hold off our celebration until he comes. God, Janet, how can we ever square it with Pete? Or maybe when you marry him he'll feel it has been worthwhile."

"We'll have to get a new staff before we can celebrate here," Janet told him. "They all walked out this morning. I thought you could mix some cocktails and then we'd go out to dinner. There's a little place I know where no one would recognize us. I go there a lot."

"It's been hell for you, too, hasn't it?" His face hardened. "Tell me about that Simmons man this morning."

"Drinks first," she said.

"All right." He looked around as though savoring his homecoming. Tonight there were no crowds outside the house; the tension was gone. "Hey, what happened to the ormolu clock? Did someone drop it?"

"I don't know."

"I never saw that crack in it before. Well, where do we keep the liquor now?" The telephone in the library rang. "That will be Pete.

I'll tell him to come along."

Cass went into the library. In a few minutes he was back, reaching for the overcoat and hat he had tossed on a chair.

"Oh, Cass," she wailed, "must you go out again?"

"He said it wouldn't take long." He flicked her a salute and the door closed behind him.

It wasn't anything. It couldn't be anything. A legal detail. Cass would return soon. And Pete. Together again. That's what she had wanted to drink to when Cass was released from Wentworth. Only forty-eight hours ago. Together again. Pete and Cass and Janet. The way it had always been.

She couldn't sit down. She paced the hall, wandered aimlessly through the drawing room, the library, the morning room. The house was terribly still. She reached out to test the lock on the garden door, to draw the draperies close together, as though something waited in the night, wanting to get in.

Nothing could happen now. They were all safe. Nothing could happen. But she could not sit still. A kind of cold dread was growing in her.

She went swiftly up the stairs to the third-floor suite where Eve and Cass had lived. It looked different now, unnaturally neat without Eve's clutter. For a moment she looked around and then she began to go through the desk in the small living room. In the drawers there was nothing but paper and envelopes and a gold pencil without any lead. The dressing table drawers were empty, so was the closet that had been crammed with Eve's clothes.

At last she got up from the crouching position in which she had peered under the bed. Where else? That was when she heard it, a faint metallic sound. The sound of a key going into a lock. The hall door between the twin houses.

Janet shot out of the suite and down the stairs to the second floor. The hall door had opened now, closed softly. There was a quiet footfall. She looked at the long flight of stairs ahead of her to the front door. She'd never make it in time. She'd be heard, caught. She opened the door of her room, closed it. There wasn't a key; she had never locked the door in her life. She leaned against it. The sound of her heart must be audible to the person who was coming down the stairs so lightly, so confidently.

She looked in despair for something with which to defend herself. The flashlight masquerading as a revolver, which Pete had given her, was still on the table in the library. The gilt telephone caught her eye. She picked it up — and remembered.

She knew what she was going to find. It had been there from the beginning, of course. Even her fear drained away in the face of the incredible, the unbearable. "Oh, Cass!" she whispered. "Oh, Cass!"

She clutched the telephone in her hand, trying to remember how it worked.

A knife was biting into her throat. Her head snapped back. Somewhere men were shouting. And Cass yelled savagely, "God damn it! Let me go!"

Her throat burned. Worse than that was the desperate struggle for breath. Janet opened her eyes. She was lying on the floor. There were lights in her room, blurred lights, a blurred figure bending over her.

Air rushed into her lungs and the blurring was gone. Lovely, sweet, reviving air. She saw clearly the man bending over her. It was Thornton with his fingers at her throat. And Janet screamed.

Behind her a breathless Mr. Potter said, "Don't let her look."

She looked, of course. Thornton had got to his feet, a thin cord dangling in his fingers. And behind him was Cass, holding a long rope with a running noose at one end.

"Was it to be suicide?" Her voice was hoarse

but it was clear. It even had a kind of detachment in it.

"That was the general idea," Cass told her.

After a look at him, the policeman holding his arm let him go. Cass turned slowly. "It's okay. I wouldn't interfere with the law. I want to see it take its course."

Still Janet did not turn her head. Not yet.

"The law will take its course," O'Toole assured him. "Caught red-handed, by God!" There was an awful delight in his voice.

And Pete Russlin, sounding spent, said, "Let's get it over with, shall we?"

Janet looked at him then. "Why Pete? Why did you do it?"

"You guessed?" Mr. Potter asked in surprise.

"Not until I heard someone in the house and started to telephone for help. I knew then. I should have known from the time when Eve said, 'The telephone,' but I misunderstood." She picked up the gilded telephone. "It's not a real phone. It's a gadget Pete brought over as a kind of private safe, because Eve was always losing her jewelry. She never locked anything up. He said no one would ever think of examining it. Then — it was just lying around — I thought she didn't want it, so I had it gilded to fit in this room to hold earrings and things like that. But,

271

somehow, I never used it."

She turned it over. "There's a trick, only I've forgotten what it is, that unlocks it — Oh, of course, the dial; it's a combination lock and Pete set it at — oh, I remember now. E-V-E." She dialed the letters and the front of the telephone sprang open on a hinge. Inside were folded half a dozen letters. She recognized Pete's writing.

"Beloved darling," the first began and ended, "Your adoring Pete." "You bewitching child," the second started and ended, "Your lover forever." "You drive me mad," the third began abruptly and ended, "No man could ever get over you."

She handed them to O'Toole with the little safe.

It was Cass who broke the silence. "I got a call from Pete. I went to his office and the place was locked, dark. I didn't like it at all. I was scared silly. I'd been framed before, so I lit out for home as fast as I could get here. I didn't know O'Toole was having the place watched. And I never thought — Janet —" His voice rose dangerously. "I can't stand much more of this. Get him out of here."

O'Toole nodded to the policeman who was holding Pete's arm.

"I'll come quietly." Pete looked at Janet. "I had to do it. God knows I didn't want to.

I had no choice."

"My best friend." At Cass's tense whisper, O'Toole stepped quickly in front of him.

Pete's face seemed to disintegrate. "I did my damnedest to save you from the chair. But you knew Eve. We were lovers from the night we met. No man who knew her could ever get her out of his system. She was poison, maybe, but, God —"

Cass stirred again. O'Toole spoke a sharp warning. Pete went out with the policeman. To the people who watched him go he seemed already a dead man.

NINETEEN

It was after two o'clock when Mr. Potter reached Graham Collinge's apartment. The latter looked over his shoulder and saw O'Toole. He grinned. "Sooner or later," he said in resignation, "I knew I'd have the police here."

"Potter said you'd still be up." O'Toole was apologetic.

"That man would say anything," Collinge retorted, but as he had left an open book on the table beside his chair, O'Toole was reassured.

The playwright poured drinks for the two men and looked at their drawn, weary faces sardonically. "Crime, to coin a phrase, does not pay."

"Right now," O'Toole assured him, "Pete Russlin is finding that out. A three-time killer and caught redhanded, by God! It doesn't happen once in a thousand times; hell, in ten thousand."

"Russlin! The lawyer who saved Cass Grant from the electric chair! I just got it over the late news, but I couldn't believe it."

"Also the guy who helped Eve Grant plan her own murder." O'Toole stretched out his

274

legs and sipped his drink. "Just one and I'm going home to bed. I've nearly forgotten what it's like."

"Not until you've talked," Collinge snarled in an unconvincing imitation of a gangster. "Russlin! And I plied him with liquor. How did you do it?"

O'Toole's eyes held an unfriendly look as he surveyed Mr. Potter. "When I think how you played me for a sucker, I ought to put you in the next cell to Russlin. Someday you're going too far."

"You had made up your mind that the Grants, one or both of them, were guilty, so I played it your way."

"And you knew it was Eve, not Janet, who had been having an affair with Russlin."

"I didn't know it was Eve, but I was almost positive. It was the only way the thing fitted. But I did know it wasn't Janet. It couldn't be."

"Will you," Collinge said in exasperation, "fish or cut bait? I am eaten up with curiosity."

O'Toole glanced at Mr. Potter but the latter was leaning back in his chair, eyes half closed.

"Well," the lieutenant said, "now you see the whole pattern the thing is clear enough. But Russlin was Cass Grant's best friend, he was presummably in love with Janet Grant, he had fought to save Cass from the chair and get him out of the state asylum. With a record like that he was simply beyond suspicion."

"But he didn't," Mr. Potter said, not bothering to open his eyes, "want Cass free. The Grants don't let go. Cass would never have rested until he had found out the truth, and Russlin was vulnerable enough, once he was suspected. There were Eve's visits to his apartment, there was his depleted bank account, and those withdrawals in cash. And — there was Simmons."

The playwright stirred. Had Russlin talked? Did they have a case?

They had a case, O'Toole assured him, and it was a beaut. An old woman in a tenement across from the warehouse had picked his picture out of a dozen they showed her. She had seen him follow Simmons into the warehouse and he never came out. And the noose Russlin had used on Simmons was like the one he had used on Eve, like the one with which he had tried to kill Janet Grant.

"Thrift, thrift, Horatio," Collinge commented. "They probably come cheaper by the dozen."

"It's your story, Potter," O'Toole said. "Why don't you tell it? After all, you had it figured out before Russlin made his statement tonight."

"He has talked then?" Collinge said in surprise. "I don't understand that. As a lawyer —"

"He was caught in the act. Four people saw him put that noose around Janet Grant's neck tonight. No man could have talked himself out of that. Anyhow, I don't think he gives a damn. He'd just like it to be over."

"If you can talk, let's see a sample," Collinge exploded.

"If O'Toole is going to talk, I'll need another drink," Mr. Potter said.

Graham Collinge refilled two glasses, looked at Mr. Potter's empty one. "Scotch with just a slight dash of arsenic?"

It started, Mr. Potter said, when Pete Russlin met Eve at a night club and lost his head about her. From that time on they were lovers. He had her number, he knew what she was, and it didn't matter. Perhaps it helped create the curious fatal attraction she had for him. He knew Frederick had priority. He knew there were occasionally other men.

Then she met Cass Grant, a wealthy young bachelor, and married him. There wasn't a damned thing Russlin could do about it.

Then Frederick persuaded her to pose

for the painting.

"There was a painting, then?" Collinge exclaimed.

"Brother!" O'Toole said feelingly.

Mrs. Frederick found the painting and threatened a scandal. Eve was scared out of her wits. She called Pete and said he had to do something quick, before Cass got involved. She didn't want that nice marriage smashed up. Pete got to the studio through a garden on 67th Street and killed Frederick.

"Why?" Collinge asked.

"Because," Mr. Potter said, "Frederick was more of a rival than Cass could ever be; Frederick was Eve's own kind; and there was Cass to take the blame. Russlin seems to have figured that he was getting rid of both his rivals at the same time, that he'd have a clear field. But he hit a piece of bad luck.

"Simmons, Eve's stepfather, had been blackmailing Frederick since he first turned Eve over to him, a year before she married Cass. He was keeping an eye on the studio and he'd taken a snapshot of that compromising picture. He saw the murder done. So when Russlin darted out of the studio — the whole thing hadn't taken more than five minutes — he found Simmons waiting for him.

"Simmons was a quick man with an idea. He'd lost one source of income, but here was another all ready for him. Why he didn't take Russlin back through the Sixty-seventh Street garden we'll never know. Probably someone came out and they couldn't afford the risk. Anyhow, they took a desperate chance and got in through the Frederick house, by that third-floor door, and later Eve let them out the front door."

"A fatal lady, all right," Collinge said. "That reminds me, what about the card left on her breast, 'My fatal lady, how do you like this wreath?' Was that coincidence?"

"That," Mr. Potter said grimly, "was Russlin. He'd visited Cass at Wentworth one day when he was reading Ovid. Russlin made some laughing remark about Cass trying to compete with Thornton and Cass said, 'Listen to this. It reminds me of Eve.' And Russlin said, 'That's odd. I've just seen a notice that she's to appear in a play called *Fatal Lady*.' After Cass was freed, Russlin had a nice link to him if he needed to use it. After all, Cass had been the fall guy once before."

Well, for four years Simmons bled Russlin white. Mr. Potter's banker persuaded Russlin's banker to talk. There were five-hundred-dollar withdrawals in cash every couple of weeks. Then Eve told Russlin she was going to marry Thornton Grant. He knew Grant would guard her like a bloodhound, that

279

this time he would lose her for good; and he'd still have Simmons around his neck for the rest of his life.

You could, O'Toole commented, almost feel sorry for the guy.

"Who could?" Collinge demanded.

Mr. Potter went on. Eve told Russlin that some of his letters to her and a print of the picture Frederick had painted were in the Grant house. She turned over her keys to him; he had them on him tonight, with a small seal with her initials in diamonds, no less, and the extra key for the third-floor door. So he went frantically through the house, trying to find the letters that could so easily incriminate him. If he cares any longer about what happens to him he must be kicking himself for not recognizing the gilded telephone as the safe he had given Eve.

Then Janet reopened the house and the danger of discovery was worse than before. Actually, Russlin had given himself away twice. Once, when he first entered the house with Janet and spoke of the crack in the or-molu clock, which had been intact when the house was closed and which he had dropped himself during one of his attempts to find the letters. The second time was when he came down the aisle after the intermission and exclaimed, "What's happened?" Obviously he thought the murder had already been discovered.

"Go on," Collinge said.

"Well," Mr. Potter said wearily, "Janet succeeded in having Cass released, Cass the patsy. And Russlin rigged up what be thought was a foolproof scheme. Eve was being driven crazy by Simmons. The time had come to eliminate him. Eve was to get the Grants to the theater, persuade Janet to go backstage on some pretext, and then Russlin would let her hear him walking with a limp. That would establish Simmons' presence. Then Simmons was to die. Janet would again claim the limping man had been on hand, and, as no one had believed her before, Cass would be properly on the spot."

"You mean Eve would have agreed to that?" Collinge was aghast.

"She took Frederick's murder in her stride," O'Toole reminded him.

"Only," Mr. Potter said, "Russlin had different ideas. Simmons was to die, but so was Eve. What was it he said tonight, O'Toole?"

"Like dope," O'Toole repeated. "She made a man an addict and he couldn't do without her. Like dope."

Well, it had worked out according to plan. Eve and Russlin between them persuaded the

Grants to go to the theater. Then Eve felt a few slight qualms. She told Russlin she had called the police and they had set up a plant in the storeroom to catch Simmons. Wouldn't it be better if they picked him up? He'd be afraid to say he'd held out on the Frederick murder. It would make him an accessory after the fact.

Russlin had a shock but he figured if he was careful he could still get away with it. Eve lured Janet backstage by hacking up a dress and Pete shot around the corner to a small bar, the Triple X, bought a bottle of Scotch, threw a bill down on the counter and cleared out. Took about three minutes for the transaction. It was no alibi, except in the theater itself, but, again, he wasn't going to be a suspect. Not with Janet and Cass set up for the slaughter.

Russlin went up the fire escape to the storeroom, put on an old raincoat he'd left there to protect himself from the plant, set down the Scotch bottle —

"How do you know?"

"Found the circular stain on the table on the stage set where he put it."

Then he waited until he heard Janet say good-by to Eve. He went down the fire escape, and began to limp. Janet went after him like a shot.

"Then he was the man she touched, not Simmons."

"He was the man she touched. When she had run into the theater, he doubled back, picked up the Scotch, dropped the raincoat, and went into Eve's dressing room. It didn't take more than two minutes to strangle her and drop the card on her breast."

"But why the card?"

"A link to Cass, one that could, reluctantly, be forced from him. Well, like nemesis, Simmons was standing in the street outside the alley. He'd seen Russlin go in and out, heard the limping step, saw Janet run after him. He knew something had happened and he was being framed.

"Next morning, after he'd read the papers, Simmons called Russlin. The receptionist, whom we hauled out of bed a couple of hours ago, overheard the call. Simmons said, 'Double trouble, double money.' Russlin had the shock of his life. So," Mr. Potter's quiet voice went out of control, steadied again, "so that's what he is going to burn for," he concluded savagely.

O'Toole looked at him, looked at Collinge. "What Russlin did," he said calmly, "was to set up an appointment with Simmons at the warehouse and then," he took an uneasy look at Mr. Potter, "then he called Janet Grant,

283

disguised his voice, and demanded money."

"So he intended Janet to take the rap," Collinge said.

"Well, Cass had landed in jail with a sound alibi and there had to be someone."

There was a long silence in the room.

O'Toole went on. "Potter had caught a glimpse of an idea. We checked at Russlin's apartment and found he'd been seeing Eve there more or less regularly for years. The pattern began to come clear. Russlin made his last bid for safety. He tried to get Janet to marry him. But she has — oh — other ideas." He buried his face in the tall glass. "Then I arrived on the scene to say that Cass was being released. So Russlin had to work fast.

"He waited until Cass reached the house, called him to his office, saw him out of the house and got in through the Frederick's. Janet was going to commit suicide. He planned to strangle her and then conceal the marks by the rope with which she was to have hanged herself. But by that time we had the picture pretty clear and we had men all around the place."

Collinge raised his glass in salute to the triumphant lieutenant. "O'Toole," he said softly, "we've got a winner."

"What have I been telling you?"

"I don't mean that. What a play! And you,

with your looks, in the leading role."

"Try it," O'Toole snarled. "Just try it."

Late the next afternoon, Mr. Potter and O'Toole, at Cass Grant's urgent request, were having drinks at the Grant house. Cass met them with hard handshakes; Janet, pale and quiet, smiled at them without speaking.

Cass grinned. "Thornton came by this morning. Last night, what with one thing and another, he had no chance to explain what he wanted. He's turning over my money as soon as the papers can be signed. Poor devil! His head kept jerking until I found myself doing it too."

"At that, he's a lucky man," O'Toole said. "Suppose he had married her!"

"Speaking of men," Janet said quickly, "and of luck, how many did you have stationed here last night?"

"One in the garden, one on the third floor, and one out in front. The man on the top floor kept ducking around while you were hunting up there."

"I haven't said thank you yet," she said. "I don't know how."

"It was Potter who gave the green light," O'Toole told her.

The long eyes looked up quickly, looked down again. "I know."

Cass raised his glass. "To both of you. Someday Janet and I will figure a way to thank you properly."

O'Toole lifted his glass. "To a new life."

"It'll be that for sure," Cass agreed. "For both of us. Janet is going to sell the shop."

"And then what?" the lieutenant asked with what Mr. Potter regarded as unnecessary curiosity.

Again Janet's long eyes were raised to Mr. Potter's face, lowered again. "I don't know."

That was when Mr. Potter began hastily to talk about taking a trip. His house was still uninhabitable. He was going south for the winter. In the late spring, perhaps, he'd drive west, see the Redwoods and Grand Canyon, the big things that help a man get life back in perspective.

He set down his glass, shook hands abruptly, and was gone almost before they realized it.

There was a little pause. Then O'Toole said quietly, "The poor devil."

"Why?" Cass asked.

"You know how I met him? I was hunting down a mass murderer and in the end it turned out to be the girl he loved. She's locked up; she'll never get out. Last I heard, her condition had deteriorated considerably. But Potter went on being in love with her.

Then," he accepted another drink, "he got over it the only normal way. He fell in love again. Now he's afraid of it; so he is running away."

"Personally," Cass declared, "I like being home. I don't care if I never leave it again."

"That's all right for the present," Janet said, a new note in her voice, "but when we've got sort of readjusted, we have things to do."

"The devil we have."

Her eyes danced. "Grand Canyon in the late spring." As Cass stared in bewilderment, she said, "You remember the toast you gave the night you came home: Unfinished business."

"You stay in there pitching," O'Toole advised her. "Maybe you can keep Potter interested, keep him too busy to get into trouble." He added dubiously, "I hope."

The employees of THORNDIKE PRESS hope you have enjoyed this Large Print book. All our Large Print books are designed for easy reading — and they're made to last.

Other Thorndike Large Print books are available at your library, through selected bookstores, or directly from us. Suggestions for books you would like to see in Large Print are always welcome.

For more information about current and upcoming titles, please call or mail your name and address to:

THORNDIKE PRESS
PO Box 159
Thorndike, Maine 04986
800/223-6121
207/948-2962